W9-BWN-859

JUST CALL MY NAME

A NOVEL BY

HOLLY GOLDBERG SLOAN

LITTLE, BROWN AND COMPANY
New York · Boston

Little, Brown and Company

Hachette Book Group
237 Park Avenue, New York, NY 10017
Visit our website at lb-teens.com

Little, Brown and Company is a division of Hachette Book Group, Inc.
The Little, Brown name and logo are trademarks of Hachette Book Group, Inc.

First Edition: August 2014

Library of Congress Cataloging-in-Publication Data

Sloan, Holly Goldberg, 1958–
    Just call my name / by Holly Goldberg Sloan. — First edition.
        pages cm
    Sequel to: I'll be there.
    Summary: The happily-ever-after that teenagers Sam and Emily envisioned for
themselves is turned on its head when Sam's unstable father makes a jailbreak and
comes after his sons and Emily for revenge.
    ISBN 978-0-316-12281-8 (hardcover) — ISBN 978-0-316-20313-5 (electronic book) —
ISBN 978-0-316-20318-0 (electronic book — library edition)   [1. Love—Fiction.
2. Fathers and sons—Fiction.   3. Family problems—Fiction.]   I. Title.
    PZ7.S633136Ju 2014
    [Fic]—dc22

                                                                            2013021599

10 9 8 7 6 5 4 3 2 1

RRD-C

Printed in the United States of America

To Robin Vera Montgomery,
Navy Wave, air traffic controller, journalist, artist,
architect, and mom…
You have always been there.

THAT WAS THEN....

The most life-changing events happen on the most ordinary days.

It was normal that his mom wasn't home. She was the one who worked, so he didn't see her much during the week.

When Sam walked through the front door, his little brother, Riddle, was in the playpen staring off at nothing as he chewed a hole in the yellow mesh designed to keep him a prisoner.

The television was on. Not cartoons but a woman selling sweaters with glittering beads all over the shoulders. No wonder the kid had his face to the wall.

The toddler was probably hungry. But he didn't ever cry for food. He wasn't that kind of baby. He should have squawked about being stuck for hours in the corner of the living room, but he usually didn't. Ever since he was born, it'd been hard to figure him out. Isn't that why they called him Riddle?

Sam's father was supposed to be waiting at the fence when school was over. But Clarence Border never showed up. Sam knew how to get home, so it didn't matter.

He was seven years old and in the second grade. Sam had no way of knowing that he'd just gone to his last day of school and would never again see his mother. He could not have imagined that the next ten years would mean living on the road.

Sam put his backpack down by the door and walked over to the playpen. Riddle didn't say anything but reached his hands straight up in the air just like the referees did on television when someone scored a touchdown.

Sam grabbed hold of his little brother's short arms and pulled him up and out of the square enclosure. Riddle was small for his age, and his wheat-colored hair and pale skin made his gray-blue eyes even more piercing. Right now they shouted gratitude.

With Riddle following behind him, Sam passed by the kitchen. He could see the leaning tower of dirty dishes in the sink, which was business as usual. As he continued down the hallway to the bedrooms, he heard his father moving something.

Sam called out: "I'm home."

No one answered.

Sam glanced into the bathroom. All of the drawers in the cabinet under the sink were open. Riddle liked to open things, so he peeled off to investigate.

In his parents' bedroom, Sam found his father stuffing clothing into two large duffel bags.

"Dad, are we going somewhere?"

His father didn't even look up.

Sam watched as his mom's jewelry box was upended into one of the two travel bags. The costume necklaces and earrings tumbled out like treasure.

4

"Go to your room and bring me your shoes. And some of Riddle's stuff."

A wave of happiness washed over the seven-year-old boy.

"Are we going to see Grandma? I wanna see Grandma!"

His father finally stopped moving long enough to acknowledge him. His eyes, Sam could see, had a jumpy look. They shifted around the room as if there were lots of people there.

Sam's happiness wave dried up.

And then, from the bathroom, came the sound of something crashing.

Riddle.

Sam got there before his father did. A blue glass dolphin that his mother had kept since she was a little girl was in pieces on the tile floor.

Riddle loved that dolphin. He always wanted to hold it like a stuffed animal—only it wasn't soft or supposed to be held. The toddler had used the open drawers as stairs to climb high enough to reach the prize.

Sam heard his father behind him, shouting, "You broke it! Are you happy now, Riddle?"

The toddler barely blinked, but Sam felt his eyes flood with tears. The shattered dolphin was Sam's fault. Riddle was his responsibility.

In one scoop his father lifted his little brother by the back of his shirt. He carried him straight outside and put him in the truck. Sam climbed in on the other side.

"I can't trust you to keep an eye on him. Now you both can just wait in here like dogs."

His father slammed the door hard and returned to the house, but he wasn't there for long. The enraged man returned in minutes with the duffel bags and a cooler. He shoved everything in the back, next to sleeping bags and a plastic tarp. There was a toolbox, and two cardboard boxes filled with jumper cables and his father's shotgun and hunting knife.

And then the motor turned over. The truck reversed, and the street disappeared from view, never to be seen again. His mother would come home hours later to an empty house that would stay that way.

Did they leave because Riddle dropped the smiling piece of blue glass? Is that what happened?

Sam Border did his best over the next ten years to forget everything about that day.

It worked.

Because now all the memories from the Day the Dolphin Broke were long gone.

THIS IS NOW....

1

Here is who we are. Imposters.

Seventeen-year-old Sam Border walked down the leafy street of the Oregon town with his little brother right at his side. And he did not once look over his shoulder. He did not crane his neck to see if anyone was following him.

But he wanted to.

Really bad.

Instead, he tried as hard as he could to appear casual, like he belonged, which of course he didn't.

His twelve-year-old brother, Riddle, walked as if he didn't have a care in the world. Which was probably the case. The kid lived in his head. Always had. Probably always would. It was what made him so different.

It was a warm June morning, and Sam realized he was sweating.

A lot.

He wanted to believe he was overheated, not flipping out.

He had to force himself to stop imagining the thousand ways his new life without Clarence Border could fall apart.

This was now a regular day. Get up. Walk over to see Emily Bell and her family.

It was that simple.

For ten years a typical day meant: Get up. Go search Dumpsters for food. Manage his father's anger. Take care of his little brother. Play his guitar until his fingertips bled. Be invisible. Watch the world go by.

But everything had changed.

Before he was numb.

Now he waited for the explosion.

Every morning until he got to Emily, he felt his stomach lurching.

For as long as he could remember, the only person who mattered in his life was Riddle. Sam had been consumed with keeping the kid safe.

Now he had a whole family to worry about.

The Bells already had two children of their own, so what could they possibly have been thinking by taking on the responsibility of him and his brother?

Their actions just didn't make sense without a motive. And so far, he couldn't uncover one.

Walking down the sidewalk, he felt that around every corner was the possibility of danger. Sam had no idea what form it would take, but this kind of happiness could never last. And that was the cause of his hidden panic.

Emily.

Focus on her.

She was his anchor.

E

MM

III

LLLL

YYYYY

Bell. Bell. Bell.

He repeated this to himself with each step.

Could something be an anchor if it wasn't weighing you down? Was it possible to be anchored to the sky?

Because that was how it felt to be with Emily: airborne. But with his feet on the ground.

She was beautiful and brilliant. She was funny and kind. She played soccer and spoke Spanish (sort of). She loved raisins and spicy mustard (not together). She laughed at the world, but most of all at herself. She loved life.

She loved *him*.

That was probably, right now, what mattered most.

His world had collided with a seventeen-year-old girl who cared. And just that simple fact had changed everything.

Sam walked faster, and a melody began to form unconsciously from the cadence of his footsteps on the concrete. The traffic whizzing by fell into a rhythm.

He found a pattern in the random motion and turned the sounds into musical notes that became a full score.

And as he did, he was able to vanish into an alternate universe where his mother had somehow survived. She hadn't been hit by a car only weeks after they'd disappeared, and he hadn't spent ten years held hostage by a crazy person.

*   *   *

Riddle looked at his big brother and knew Sam was thinking about Emily.

That's what Sam did all the time. He worked on his music, and he got gooey about his girlfriend.

Riddle had his own new love affair going now. With chicken. And the thought of it consumed him.

There were so many ways to cook a hen. Until recently, he never knew you could bake it or fry it or boil it or barbecue it. And it could be served at many different temperatures.

Debbie Bell let him in the kitchen whenever he wanted.

His preferred routine had three parts:

First he helped cook. Then he ate. And finally he drew the dish in a sketchbook that he kept with him at all times. The pictures took as much time to do as some of the meals.

There was only one major stumbling block for him when it came to advancing in the world of food preparation.

Words.

He couldn't read. He knew about letters, of course. He'd learned their shapes and some of their sounds, mostly from road signs. But he had never gone to school, and he had trouble putting it all together.

That meant he was twelve years old and still on the outside looking in.

Emily Bell's toes were curling and uncurling in her flip-flops, and she couldn't make them stop. Her digits had gone rogue.

She had to stand up to regain control of her own body.

She still got *that* excited to see him.

And then...two figures appeared. Far in the distance, but Emily was certain of who they were.

Riddle was a kid. But he didn't have the distracted quality of a typical twelve-year-old boy. He seemed both older and younger at the same time.

Right now he appeared to be walking on his tiptoes. Maybe she was imagining that. But he was bouncy.

At his side was Sam.

She didn't have her glasses on. Or her contact lenses. But it didn't make a difference. She knew.

He was tall. Not muscle-bound, but strong. His thick hair, even when cut short, had a mind of its own.

But that wasn't how she was certain it was Sam. It was the way he moved.

He didn't stride forward with teenage-boy confidence. But he didn't cower either.

The fact was that his feet didn't touch the ground like other people's.

She realized now that something in the horror of their life with their crazy father had made Sam and his little brother walk without leaving footprints.

Riddle went inside the house, and Emily and Sam took a seat on the wicker sofa on the front porch, draping their bodies over each other like two blankets. The first thing they did every morning was take the time to get caught up.

"My dad made another appointment to see the adoption lawyer."

Sam nodded as she continued.

"Apparently, the best option is for my parents to become your legal guardians. But to start the process to adopt Riddle."

Sam could feel himself relax just being in her presence. He said:

"'Legal guardian' sounds good. We don't want to be brother and sister."

"No. Too weird."

Sam knew the answer, but he still asked the question. "And adopting Riddle is the right thing?"

They had gone over this many times, but she was patient. "It protects him. Not just health insurance and the legal stuff, but in all the other ways. If you weren't about to be eighteen, my mom would be pushing for you to do it, too."

Emily squeezed his arm and was surprised by how firm it felt. It wasn't only that he had muscles. He was tense. She could hear that in the tightness in his voice, but this was further proof.

The thought that he was on shaky ground made something inside Emily shift. She was no kind of hero. Her first response, even when she heard just a firecracker, was to run.

But when it came to Sam and Riddle Border, that changed.

She became fierce.

They weren't just deserving of love. They were different. They had been victims of abuse, and despite that, the two boys were more in touch with simple kindness than anyone she'd ever known.

Emily was going to be there for them. Always. Forever.

*　　*　　*

Sam looked over and saw something in her eyes and he knew that she was now worrying about him.

That was no good.

She believed in being positive. About everything. It was almost irritating. He tried now to say the right thing.

"I'll be eighteen on my birthday. Then I won't even need the guardian part."

"No. You'll be a college student—"

Sam interrupted her. They'd been over this many times, but it still didn't compute.

"It's hard for me to see how I'm going from second grade to college."

"You'll be in the music department. And obviously there are special circumstances. You tested really well—remember?"

Sam tried not to wince. The thought of that day of testing was still a nightmare.

He and Riddle had been taken by Emily's parents to see an educational specialist. Sam was anxious. Riddle had no anxiety about the whole experience. And then he was the one who came up short.

Sam's little brother could barely make out the words in the picture-book reader for first graders.

Was it Sam's fault Riddle couldn't read? Shouldn't Sam have at least taught his brother that? All those hours sitting in a truck? He'd failed the kid. Big-time.

Sam pushed aside the avalanche of guilt and said, "I guess I just start by getting through summer school."

Emily nodded. "Exactly."

Sam's eyes shifted and he found himself now staring intently across the street at nothing more than a hedge.

Emily wrapped her left leg around his right calf. He could feel himself relax as he said:

"I'm trying, Emily."

"I know you are. And you're doing great."

Sam's head sank deeper into the pillow. When he was with Emily, he was doing great.

It was when he *wasn't* with her that was the problem.

He mumbled, "What's the thing you keep telling me?"

Emily scrunched up her nose. She looked so beautiful when she was really serious. He was still in the stage where every change of expression on her face seemed fascinating. Would that go away? He hoped not.

"Trust the unknown."

"Right."

Emily rolled over onto her side and looked right at him. "You don't need to be afraid anymore. About anything, Sam."

Sam didn't even think. He just answered. "I'm afraid of the future."

"And why is that?"

Sam pulled her close. "Before, I had nothing to lose."

2

Clarence Border smiled at the woman.

She was reading his file, so she didn't see. He'd grin again when she looked up. But nothing too committed. He didn't want to seem desperate.

Because he was way past desperate, into some other territory of distress.

Can a man in a state prison, facing multiple charges ranging from kidnapping to fraud to larceny, be anything else?

The public defender put down the file and said:

"You took your two sons from their home ten years ago. That much you don't dispute—am I correct?"

It was then that she saw his toothy expression.

He realized immediately it was bad timing. He had only twenty minutes with the woman, and seduction was probably the wrong approach.

"Yes. But I'm innocent. You get that—right? I did nothing but be a good parent to those kids."

The woman didn't blink.

"I think our best chance involves a plea bargain."

He sat up straighter in his chair. He needed to get her to listen. To understand. To be on his side.

"But—I'm innocent."

"Your sons have given extensive testimony that when they were no longer of use to you, you tried to kill them."

"I didn't—"

"You aimed. You fired the weapon. There is evidence."

Clarence could feel his whole body twist, from the top of his skull to the toes on both of his feet. Even the foot that was no longer there.

He exhaled.

Slowly.

And then:

"They are liars. Both of them. That's the first thing you need to understand."

The woman looked back at the file. And he knew she had made up her mind way before she got in the cinder-block room with the sticky plastic chairs and the smell of ammonia.

New angle. Not victim. Stronger than that. He continued:

"I'd like to talk to you about what really happened."

He shut his eyes so that he could concentrate. And then he slowly began:

"I was the stay-at-home dad. And there was a fight with the wife. She wanted us to leave. All of us. She asked for that. She said she needed time away from the kids and me. I gave her a huge opportunity when I accepted the responsibility of raising the boys on my own. I was a single parent. That's not easy."

Clarence opened his eyes and hoped he looked incredibly sincere as he said:

"Do you have any children?"

The woman spoke ice chips:

"I'm here to give you the best possible legal advice. Right now, if convicted, you face a lifetime in jail. You understand that—am I correct?"

Clarence tried to stay on track.

"We traveled. Me and the boys. We moved a lot because work is hard to find. There weren't problems until we got to Oregon. That's when my oldest boy met a girl. That's what caused the trouble. Her family turned my boys against me. They are the ones who should be sitting here today—not me!"

Her answer said it all: "You are going to trial. Not the people who stepped in to help your sons."

He got up from the table. *Help my sons?* Those people were the kidnappers. Not him.

They'd get their due.

That was all he knew for certain as he abruptly left the room.

*   *   *

Prison is a place where there is never, ever silence.

At all hours of the day and night, sound ricochets off the

hard surfaces in an assault that literally makes people's eardrums bleed.

Mixed in with radios blaring and toilets flushing, carts are rolling and mattresses are slamming. Layered on top of that bed of constant clatter are raging arguments between groups of men and between men and their souls.

Someone is always shouting.

And someone is always wailing. Half the time, the rant is directed at a blank wall.

What Clarence Border really needed was for the noise to stop. And it didn't.

The way he saw it, there was no public defender on the planet who was going to do the right thing, which meant that by the time the system was finished with him, he'd be eligible for parole when he was 213 years old.

His two no-good, backstabbing sons would probably be dead by then.

He hoped so.

Just thinking of Sam and Riddle made everything worse.

He'd seen the house that belonged to the Bell family. He could imagine the kind of kitchen they had and the food they ate.

And now, lying on his back and trying hard to make the pain go away in a foot that wasn't even there, he thought about the budget for three meals of inmate food: two dollars a day.

There were glass bits and sand, hair, and even parts of rodents in the slop that he was given to eat.

He'd be much happier if they just gave him a large box of

saltine crackers and a glass of water. It wouldn't be cruel and unusual punishment. He loved those crackers.

Clarence could see Sam and Riddle sitting at a real table, eating off fancy plates and using silver utensils.

He scraped his spork across the molded plastic plate that tasted like ammonia from the dishwashing dunk.

Both of his boys now probably had their own bathrooms with stacks of fresh towels waiting after they took long, steamy showers.

He had no privacy and only the constant smell of sewage and sweat mixed with the glare of the twenty-four-hour fluorescent lights overhead.

He was subjected to the contempt of the guards, the harassment of the other inmates, and the pain of his physical condition.

And all that made a noise that buzzed nonstop in his head. It was a chain saw of fury directed at his own flesh and blood.

Well, he was going to settle the score.

Clarence held his hands out in front of his face and stared at his fingers.

He'd read in a magazine that researchers at the University of Alberta had determined that the shorter a man's index finger when compared to his ring finger, the greater his tendency to exhibit aggressive behavior.

And by *aggressive*, they meant violent.

It turned out (according to these eggheads) that the length of your fingers had to do with how much testosterone you were exposed to in the womb.

That's what fueled all the Mr. Short-Index-Fingers (short, at least, compared to their ring fingers) to become Mr. Hotheads.

Clarence smiled. On both of his hands, his ring fingers were much longer than the digits right next to his thumbs.

It was strangely comforting to know that he was born who he was. Not every man could swing a shovel and hit someone squarely in the face. Just like most guys couldn't take a pair of pliers and rip off someone's ear.

Clarence didn't need to be provoked to do these things. He could unleash his rage machine at will.

His two boys didn't have that kind of power inside. They were, he knew for certain, made of other stuff.

Clarence shut his eyes and was able to picture Sam playing the guitar. Wasn't that all the kid had ever done, from the time he could first hold the instrument?

Riddle used his hands to draw. He usually didn't have paper or the right pens, but he still found a way. The kid was left-handed, which made sense to Clarence because the boy approached everything from the wrong side.

Clarence held his hand in front of his face and felt himself ignite. He bolted up from his thin mattress and screamed.

It was a full-on, mouth-open, high-pitched cry. The sound was a mix of anger, fear, and pain.

When it was over, he sank back down and waited for someone to come check on him.

But no one did. Because not a person on this earth cared how he was doing.

And that was a feeling worse than being locked up.

3

Everything in the kitchen now had a yellow sticky tag with a word written on it.

Refrigerator. Stove. Sink. Counter. Table. Clock. Towel. Wall. Coffeemaker. Vitamins. Knives. Ladle. Spatula.

Jared found it creepy. He was ten years old, and all kinds of things were now driving him crazy. Of course Riddle couldn't read. That made sense. But why was Jared's mother spending every minute of every day trying to make up for lost time?

The way Jared saw it, Riddle didn't need a tutor three times a week. And he certainly didn't need the world labeled. Jared wasn't going to wear a tag that said Brother, even if they paid him.

The whole house was starting to look like it was part of some kind of estate sale, only there were no prices on the big labels.

And then his big sister made a discovery. "Mom...have you noticed that Riddle has to get up really close to your stickers to see the letters? And he squints a lot."

Debbie Bell glanced across the room. Riddle was drawing a picture of a pot roast on his new art pad. His nose was almost touching the paper.

Debbie Bell had taken Riddle and Sam for physicals, and Riddle was being treated for asthma. Now she looked puzzled. "Dr. Howard didn't say anything about his vision."

Emily shrugged. "Maybe he didn't check it."

Two days later, Riddle was diagnosed as being nearsighted, with extreme astigmatism in his left eye. Because Debbie Bell had to work that day at the hospital, Emily, Sam, and Riddle went to the optometrist's office together to pick out glasses. They asked Jared to come, but he'd made it clear that it was the last thing he wanted to do.

Emily headed for the section marked *Juvenile Boys*. But Riddle had his own ideas. There was a photo of a redheaded girl wearing rectangular orange glasses. He pointed to the image. "I want those."

Sam looked from the photo back to his little brother. "Riddle, I think those might be for girls."

That made Riddle laugh. "How can there be different glasses for girls and boys?"

Emily whispered to Sam with concern: "He's never experienced peer pressure."

Sam and Emily tried to talk Riddle into at least looking at the other choices, but when the kid set his mind to something, there was no changing it.

A week later they returned when the glasses were ready. Emily stared at Riddle's reflection in the mirror. He suddenly looked like he was from the punk-rock scene in London in the late 1970s. He was now somehow the hippest person in any room.

When Riddle spun around from the optometrist to face them, he could see Emily and Sam, and his eyes lit up as a smile stretched across his face. "I see you guys! Everything is so much bigger!"

Riddle's head swung in all directions. "I see all the little things. I feel dizzy because I can see so much."

He was laughing now. He turned back toward Emily and Sam. "Guys—I really see you!"

Sam shut his eyes and tried not to feel anything. But when he glanced over at Emily, he could see that she, too, had a wobbly grin on her face.

Happiness.

The emotion that frightened him so much.

* * *

Summer officially started two days later.

Sam began a program at Baine College designed to acclimate students with learning differences who would be new in the fall. He wasn't dyslexic, like the majority of the other kids in this summer class. He had his own unique issues.

Sam had no formal training or instruction from a teacher. He'd followed no curriculum. He had no experience as a student since grade school.

Emily's father was a music professor at Baine. So obviously the place was making allowances. That put Sam even more on edge.

He now sat in the very back of the classroom, convinced that the twenty-two (he counted them) other students could see that he had not been in school since he was seven years old.

He was certain they could tell that he had no idea what to say, when to write something down, or even how to listen.

It was torture.

A woman came in and, with a marker, wrote DR. JULIA HUNT in block letters on the whiteboard. Sam kept his eyes glued to her as she spoke about the requirements for the class. He could see people typing into computers that they'd suddenly pulled from backpacks and placed on their desks.

It was impossible for him to listen to what the woman said and at the same time try to take down notes. And he didn't have a computer. Even if he did, he had no idea how to type.

He could see other students tapping rapidly. It was as if they were playing an instrument. Their wrists stayed planted on the keyboard while their fingertips bobbled up and down.

Dr. Julia Hunt was talking now about the books they would read and the papers they would write. And in the end, there would be a final. But she didn't say a final what.

Just a final.

And she said that the final would count for 50 percent of the grade. She looked very serious. She was the judge and the jury and the executioner.

Then Dr. Julia Hunt began to call names. Like a lineup. Like a firing squad.

Sam watched as the other students answered. They said only, "Here." A few names were met with silence. And then the woman said:

"Sam Border."

Sam felt like the temperature in the room had risen ten degrees in a matter of seconds. But he was able to open his mouth and get out a single word.

He said, "Yes."

No one laughed, and the woman was on to another name as he shut his eyes.

Against all odds, he had survived.

*   *   *

On Sam's first day, Emily had her second shift as a bus girl at Ferdinand's Fine French Restaurant on Oak Street.

Like Sam, she felt as if she were on another planet.

Because she also had no idea what she was doing.

In the restaurant's kitchen, Emily was responsible for sorting the dirty dishes and cutlery in order for the two dazed-looking guys (with the steamy water hoses that slung down from metal arms on the ceiling) to load up the forever-chugging dishwashing machines.

She had to keep the water glasses topped off in the dining room. And a constant supply of warm bread going out in the wicker baskets that all the diners got when they first sat down.

It was her duty to reset each table and deal with the linens and all of the garbage after every shift.

It didn't sound like that big a deal when she'd first heard the duties, but she quickly learned that there was a lot more going on in a restaurant than meets the eye.

And on her second day on the job, she had the biggest screwup anyone could remember happening at Ferdinand's.

The restaurant was in an old brick building, and while it had been renovated, there were things that dated back seventy-five years, to when the place had been some kind of beer hall.

Emily had been told multiple times to hit the switch by the entrance before she went inside the walk-in freezer. The toggle activated a red light over the heavy metal door, signifying that someone was inside the cooler.

The door was tricky. Sometimes it was accidentally left partway open, and the cold air escaped. But when it was closed hard, the mechanism that released from the inside had been known to malfunction.

And on that fateful day, in the middle of lunch service, Emily was in a hurry when she entered the walk-in to get more butter. Natalie, the daytime hostess, passed through the kitchen. She saw that the red light wasn't on and assumed that the freezer door had been left open.

So she put her shoulder to the metal and shoved hard until it clicked.

Inside, the vacuum seal of the door made a sucking sound. Emily shouted: "Hey!"

It was so cold in the walk-in that she could see her breath as a white puff.

The "hey" now lingered in the air. Emily put the butter tray down and went to the metal door and pushed. Nothing. She then beat on the only exit with her fist.

"I'm locked in here! *Help!*"

The ceilings and walls and door in the freezer were six inches thick, made from insulated foam covered in stainless steel. The floor was a sheet of aluminum. A heavy plastic curtain hung in front of the doorway.

It was an extremely cold, sealed, metal box lit by a single weak lightbulb.

The temperature inside was negative two degrees Fahrenheit.

After Emily pounded on the door for what seemed like an eternity but was only eighteen seconds, she knew that she was in trouble.

The whirling fans of the cooling units made such a racket that she could barely hear her own knocking on the inside, so forget anyone hearing on the other side of the metal.

Emily's uniform consisted of a sleeveless white shirt and a wraparound black skirt. Her legs were bare, and on her feet she wore gold ballet slippers.

She had been inside the walk-in icebox for less than a minute and she was already freezing. Emily felt her breath turn shallow as she realized that she was light-headed. It was possible, she suddenly realized, that she might faint.

There was a box of frozen imported anchovies behind her, and Emily sank down onto it, taking a seat in the dark corner as she folded her head down into her knees.

And then suddenly the freezer door was flung open. Emily opened her eyes to hear a voice say, "She's not in here."

Emily tried to get to her feet, but it was too late.

The woozy feeling returned as the room swirled, and she had no choice but to drop back down to the anchovies as the freezer door slammed shut.

4

Clarence lay on his cot and stared at the cement ceiling. Why had he taken the two boys in the first place?

All those years ago, he could have just walked out the door, suitcase in hand, and never come back.

Wouldn't that have been so much easier?

But the voices in his head had told him that a man with little kids automatically looked trustworthy. They allowed him to blend into a crowd. And the older one, even at seven, had a brain. He was useful.

Clarence took them because they gave him power. They said that he was in charge. And that felt good. Until they stopped listening.

Is that what happened?

No.

They met a family. And those people turned his boys against him.

Somewhere in Clarence's cell block, an inmate was chanting. He was saying over and over again:

"The worst thing to happen is the best thing to happen."

That guy fixated on phrases and then spent not just hours but whole days repeating them.

At very high volume.

For a whole week, the guy wouldn't shut up about hot sauce.

Now the lunatic's new words bored into Clarence's head. The voice became his interrogator.

What was the worst thing to happen to him?

Being sent to jail.

And how did that happen?

His sons had turned against him. And when he tried to even the score, he'd been attacked by his oldest. He'd been injured up there on the mountain. His leg had broken from the fall, and an infection had set in. At least that's what they claimed later, when the doctor in the hospital amputated below the knee.

So maybe the worst thing to happen was the surgery?

He could feel his missing toes, his once bony ankle, and his always flat instep. He reached out to touch the phantom body part, and his fingers, moving through air, touched real nerves in the emptiness.

All the while he heard: "The worst thing to happen is the best thing to happen."

And the words turned into a plan.

5

Emily was in the freezer for almost three hours.

During that time, in an attempt to keep warm, she removed the dish towel that was in her skirt pocket and wrapped it around her head. She then placed a shallow bucket over the dishrag.

As the cold got worse Emily took her knife and cut down the insulated curtain that was in front of the door. She then wrapped herself in the thick piece of plastic and pulled her knees up to her chest.

She was turning into a human Popsicle.

To keep from doing something irrational, she started to sing. She sang the same song over and over and over again.

And she thought of Sam.

It was their song. And she didn't sing it well. For the last hour, she hummed, only managing a few words:

"Just call my name . . . and I'll be there."

*   *   *

No one in the restaurant knew where the new bus girl had gone.

The hostess said it was possible Emily had quit. All anyone could say was that she'd disappeared at some point before the beef bourguignonne ran out.

Finally, with lunch service over, Juan Ico signed for an order of frozen halibut from the seafood delivery service.

It needed to go right into the walk-in.

Juan put the boxes on a handcart, and when he opened the freezer door, he found himself staring down at Emily. She had a bucket on her head. A gray curtain was wrapped around her shivering body and was gripped by blue fingers.

His scream was heard on the sidewalk outside.

As Emily was carried into the dining room, she saw a sign over the kitchen door. It looked as if it had been there for many years.

It read:

Be alert. Be aware. Be alive.

* * *

No matter how many times he asked, most people called him by his old name: Bobby Ellis.

But that person was gone.

Because Bobby Ellis had died at the Churchill High School prom at the Mountain Basin Inn when the girl he was obsessed with walked out on him.

Emily Bell had been Bobby Ellis's date on the evening he

should have only been celebrating that he had been crowned prom king.

It was epic.

Just not in a good way.

Bobby Ellis had suffered first-degree sunburn earlier in the day. He had then been pulled over in his car for speeding. He had a fender bender, followed by a spray-on-tan mishap in which he cut his knee in the stall and was sent to the hospital for stitches.

The daylight portion of his catastrophe concluded when his big toe broke after he kicked a bathroom wall.

His parents had to drive him and Emily to the prom. And only an hour later, she walked out on him. The night ended with Bobby Ellis drinking so much that he was taken back to the hospital on a stretcher.

His crown, and most of his pride, got lost along the way.

Bobby decided after that to make this the summer he would have a fresh start. With everything in his life.

He started with his name.

Bobby Ellis asked people to now call him Robb. He spelled it with two *b*'s.

Done.

So far the only people who got the name right worked at the Hair Asylum, which was where Robb Ellis got his hair cut. The salon was located on Oak Street, just down from Ferdinand's Fine French Restaurant. (The name of the dining establishment rubbed him the wrong way. Were there French restaurants that served coarse French food? He didn't think so.)

Robb had vowed to himself to keep his distance from Emily Bell.

She had her life with the mysterious boy from nowhere. And Robb had his. Once they'd shared secrets. Now he found it hard to even look at her.

Or at least that's what he thought until he saw an ambulance in front of Ferdinand's.

Hadn't Emily's best friend, Nora, said Emily had a summer job there? He had tried not to pay attention, but he was certain now. Yes. That's where she was working.

Robb picked up his pace and met the two paramedics on the sidewalk. His mother was a detective. He was used to law enforcement and disasters, and he easily wedged himself between the two men. "What kind of emergency you got going on?"

The larger of the two medics, the one carrying the orange EMS case, said, "Possible hypothermia."

It was eighty-five degrees outside. Everyone was wearing shorts and sleeveless shirts. Robb rolled his eyes.

"C'mon, guys."

Now it was the shorter one who spoke:

"He's serious. A girl locked herself in the freezer."

Robb's eyebrows rose.

"Wow. On purpose?"

The medics blew past him into the restaurant, and Robb just naturally followed at their heels.

*　*　*

Inside, a half dozen people were gathered around a shape stretched out on the carpeted floor.

37

White tablecloths covered the body. There were no blankets in the restaurant, and as it was summer, no one had brought a coat to work.

The small group cleared to let the emergency medical technicians take charge, and it was then that Robb Ellis saw who was causing the problem.

"Emily..."

Her face was gray, and her lips were blue.

Robb Ellis found the look incredibly attractive. It was sort of like vampire makeup or something.

"Bobby...?"

Emily saw him and tried to sit up. He could see that the look on her face said: *What are you doing here?*

But she pulled herself forward too fast, and her body temperature was too low, and so was her blood sugar.

Emily hadn't eaten since breakfast, and now it was three in the afternoon. The room started to spin, and then her vision started to pixelate and she dropped back to the carpet.

And Robb Ellis took it all as a good sign.

*   *   *

Leo Saar, the owner of the restaurant, was in a foul mood.

It was never good for business to have an ambulance with swirling lights parked in front of an eating establishment. For some people that's all it took to trigger a decade of irrational dining fear.

So now Leo had that to worry about.

38

The girl had looked so trouble-free when he'd hired her. What if the halibut hadn't arrived, and no one had gone inside the freezer, and she'd gone ice block on him?

Leo tried to shake it off. He was happy that the other kid had showed up. The tall teenager wanted to go with Emily in the ambulance, which took the burden off the restaurant to send an employee.

So that's why Leo had offered the guy a job.

Now he looked at the slip of paper where the kid had written his contact information.

Robb Ellis.

Leo was going to have him start on Monday.

6

Sam walked out of Addison Hall and felt only one thing: relief.

He had been, he now realized, filled with dread because of summer school. But now he'd attended a college class. And survived.

He walked to the parking lot, smiling. He was one big happy face. The sun was golden warm. The trees were waving green. Not a cloud in the sky, just blue. Blue. Blue.

Joy.

That's what he felt. And then his cell phone rang.

"Sam, this is Debbie...."

He heard something in her voice.

"What's wrong?"

The sun suddenly felt relentlessly harsh. The trees were sick or something, because the leaves now rattled. And the sky came falling down.

"Emily's fine. But she's at the hospital."

"Hospital" was all he heard.

* * *

Sam remembered nothing about the drive.

Debbie Bell said three times that he shouldn't worry. But her words were meaningless.

He'd known something bad was going to happen, but Sam never thought it would be that the girl who'd changed his entire life would freeze to death.

Emily didn't succumb to the elements during her three hours in a minus-two-degree walk-in freezer, but only because she had done everything right, including not panic.

Now Sam was doing that for her.

He had been right all along.

This new world would come apart.

* * *

He found her under a flesh-colored electric blanket. She was hooked up to two machines that were monitoring something. Sam stood just inside the opening in the curtain, which surrounded the hospital bed.

Emily's eyes were shut.

His first thought was that it wasn't her. She was blue. Maybe it was the lights. No. It was her skin. Her circulation was that messed up.

All he could think was that this couldn't be Emily, because she looked so small and so fragile.

But he didn't move, because it was possible that any

41

moment the machines keeping her alive would stop and the room would burst into flames.

As he waited for that to happen, her eyes opened, and they focused on him. There was no doubt that it was Emily.

Sam tried to say something, but nothing came out. He couldn't lose it right in front of her.

So he just stared.

Unblinking.

For way too long.

His throat had closed up. He could have said, *How are you?* He tried to say, *Are you okay?* But instead, in a tumble of words more heartfelt than he'd ever expressed, he managed, "I love you."

It came out too loud. And no doubt desperate, because he could see her expression change. She was alarmed. Was he scaring her?

"Sam. It's all right. I'm okay."

Her hand slid out from underneath the warming blanket as he stepped to the bed. His fingers wrapped around hers, which were cold to the touch. Tears suddenly spilled from his eyes like rain. Unstoppable.

Sam stood next to the bed. What could he say that might comfort her? "I—"

But she stopped him.

"It was all my fault. I didn't press the red light. No one knew I was in there."

Sam climbed up onto the hospital gurney. The electric blanket had wires, and so did her left arm, but he was careful as he found a way to thread his arms around her and hold her close.

And there they lay.

Together.

It was noisy and the intercom sounded every few minutes, but being joined brought a kind of relief that found both of them, only moments later, asleep.

*   *   *

He woke to the sound of the curtain shifting along the rod that encircled the bed, and then a male voice said:

"Oh. Sorry. I don't wanna interrupt or anything."

Sam looked over his shoulder. Emily's voice was a thin whisper:

"Sam, this is Bobby Ellis."

The teenage boy glanced from Emily to Sam.

"Robb. Not Bobby. It's Robb now. I changed it."

Sam suddenly felt foolish in the hospital bed. He pulled back the electric blanket and swung his legs down to the lino-leum floor. What was this guy doing here?

Emily had explained to Sam before that Bobby Ellis had helped her in the past. Now she was in the emergency room, and somehow this old boyfriend, or whatever he was, was standing there. He was part of this.

"I was just walking by the restaurant and I saw the ambulance. It was a crazy coincidence."

Sam was surprised to hear himself say, "Emily doesn't believe in coincidence. She believes everything is fate."

He regretted the words as soon as they were out of his mouth, because Emily instantly looked hurt.

Her voice was insistent. "No...all kinds of stuff can be random. I just think that sometimes unplanned things can matter."

Sam's eyes moved from Emily to Robb Ellis, and he couldn't stop himself from wondering how he would make their lives different.

*　*　*

Clarence dedicated every minute in his cell to documenting his prison abuse. When the newly assigned lawyer next came to visit to discuss the upcoming trial, Clarence demanded expert medical care.

Henry Peacor had too many cases and not enough time to deal with his clients. And so he took on interns. He now had an office full of them.

Henry was instructed to focus on Clarence Border's physical condition. He needed the kind of nerve testing that wasn't going to happen in the infirmary behind the walls of the maximum-security prison.

The interns took care of everything. They sent e-mails and repeatedly called the American Civil Liberties Union. They contacted Human Rights Watch. They launched a Facebook page and opened a Twitter account with the single purpose of making an inmate's physical plight a social issue. They cut together a compelling video. They even suggested that they might stage a hunger strike.

Together, Henry's legal interns began to build a case

describing a man with an amputated leg, in extreme pain, improperly fitted with a prosthetic device that was the equivalent of torture.

As Clarence explained, his leg was a Bill of Rights issue.

Because as written, the Eighth Amendment states that "excessive bail shall not be required, nor excessive fines imposed, *nor cruel and unusual punishments inflicted.*"

And denying a prisoner proper medical care was cruel and unusual punishment.

It just was.

7

After Emily almost froze to death, Sam went every day after summer school to meet her at Ferdinand's. He couldn't stand the idea of his girlfriend being in the world without the protection of his watchful eye.

It didn't matter that he never knew when her shift would end. What was important was that he was watching there for her.

And then Destiny appeared on the sidewalk in front of the restaurant.

The girl was a little pixie of a thing.

She had on a short-short pink skirt and an oversize man's dress shirt. She wore pointy orange slippers that came from Thailand and were not meant to ever touch the pavement.

Her hair, which was dyed the color of a blond baby's—all shiny white—was piled up on her head and held in place by an ornamental chopstick. Little dark roots were visible at the base of her scalp.

The girl stared at Sam and said, "You look hot. If you're

going to be waiting for long, you can come hang out in the shop." Her head tilted over to the door of a store called the Orange Tree.

Sam looked around. Was she talking to him?

The girl continued. "I saw you out here yesterday with the dark-haired girl from the French place."

Now Sam knew for certain that she was speaking to him. He remained silent, but that didn't stop her.

"I'm Destiny. Destiny Verbeck. I've got a job in there. It's a whole-lot-of-nothing shop."

Sam nodded and then hoped it didn't look like he was agreeing with what she'd just said.

"We sell cards and T-shirts and toys that adults think kids would like, but they don't. It's all expensive junk, really. I mean just useless. But people buy it. Earrings made from bottle caps. Toilet paper with your fortune printed on one side. It's just a bunch of crap."

Destiny pulled on her skirt, not down but up, making it even shorter. She then continued. "We sell something called Earthquake-in-a-Can. You hit a button, and it shakes. Battery-powered. If that's not junk, I don't know what is."

Destiny wiggled her toes in her tiny orange slippers and rocked back and forth on her heels. "We've got a couch in the store. You may as well come inside and waste your time talking to me."

Sam wasn't talking to her. But she didn't seem to need any encouragement to carry on the conversation. She peered at him and suddenly seemed very serious.

"What did you say your name was again?"

He hadn't said. Because he had yet to open his mouth. Now he did as he answered: "Sam."

Destiny repeated it, and the word seemed to have two syllables.

"SSSSee-Aam. I like that. It fits you. It's nice when that happens. I was born Amber, but I changed my name to Destiny. Amber didn't work for me. It was too, I don't know, 'boring girl.'"

She was moving now, and Sam felt that he had no choice but to follow as she continued:

"I just wasn't an Amber. But Destiny works. Everyone remembers it. You will, too. I guarantee it. Tonight, when you're just about to fall asleep, you'll think, *What happened to me today?* And then it will come to you. Destiny!"

And then she headed into the Orange Tree, and Sam found himself right behind the short-short pink skirt and the little orange slippers.

It was times like this, he decided, when it would have been a good thing to know more about girls.

Like how do you politely get away from one?

*   *   *

Destiny Verbeck might have looked like she could play the part of a baby wood nymph in a professional ice show, but she was tough.

She had to be.

Her mother had died of a drug overdose after being clean and sober for four years. Her one slipup ended it all.

After that, eleven-year-old Destiny, known up until that point as Amber, changed her name.

In a kinder world, Destiny's father, while still grieving, would have stepped in to raise her.

If Ronnie Verbeck had lived a hundred years earlier, he would have been a horse thief. Instead, he ran a ring of crooks who only stole newish Hondas from Vegas hotel parking lots. Ronnie Verbeck knew how to ship a stripped sedan south of the border in less than six hours.

Only two months after his wife died, Ronnie was caught in a government sting that led to his conviction. He named names, giving up as many members of the stolen-car ring as possible, but it wasn't enough. He still found himself behind bars.

No one on either side of the family came forward. And that left Amber-turned-Destiny Verbeck in the hands of foster care.

Four families and five years later, she walked out the front door of a house in Boise, Idaho, and didn't look back.

She was almost sixteen, and she'd had enough of the spin cycle of schools, makeshift families, and disappointment. Despite all the obstacles that had been thrown in front of her, she knew that she could make it on her own.

A man named Wynn Lappe married Destiny on her birthday in Billings, Montana. He was twenty-seven years old and drove trucks for a living. He thought she was twenty-three.

Destiny didn't have a commercial driver's license, but

she learned to drive a big rig. An eighteen-wheeler requires nerves of steel when you don't know what you're doing, and she had those, even though turning sharp corners still presented some problems for her.

Destiny traveled with Wynn for a year, seeing thousands and thousands of miles of moving blacktop and not a lot else. Wynn was fundamentally decent but also tragically boring. At least to a teenager with big dreams.

And that was why Destiny left him at a truck stop in Lebo, Kansas, hopping a ride with another driver while Wynn slept in the upper bunk of the big rig, above the cab.

She left a note saying she was sorry that it was over. She hoped he'd file the paperwork for a divorce, but if he didn't, she'd understand.

Now, eight months later, the girl was working at the Orange Tree gift shop in an Oregon college town. She'd been there only a few days, and already the place seemed dreary.

And then she saw Sam.

* * *

With the tall boy at her heels, she pointed to the purple sofa next to the greeting-card display. "Take a load off. You can see the sidewalk, and you'll know when your girlfriend comes out of the restaurant."

Sam did everything he could not to look at Destiny's short-short pink skirt as he awkwardly folded his lanky body onto the couch.

Destiny Verbeck was petite and very, very, very pretty. But she was too tiny to be called beautiful, because even wearing heels she still looked like a kid.

"I know I look young, but I'm twenty. Just turned."

Destiny took a stool that was behind the cash register and pulled it around to the front of the counter so that she could be closer to Sam.

She hopped up onto the seat (and then crossed her legs, which caused her skirt to rise up another inch), sighing as if she'd just climbed ten flights of stairs.

"Have you ever worked in a gift shop? You wouldn't believe how boring it is. I mean, it's watching-paint-dry time in here. Just having someone else around makes it easier."

Sam wondered what he needed to do to make her stop talking, and then a bell sounded on the door and a woman in her thirties entered the store. Destiny eyed her with obvious hostility.

The woman picked up a blue-and-white polka-dot hair accessory and held it in the air as she called out, "How much is the headband?"

Destiny made a face. "Two things to know before we talk price. The first is that those headbands give you a headache about five minutes after you put one on. I know. I tried to wear one yesterday. And the second thing is that they're made of some piece-of-crap plastic underneath the fabric, because they snap in two like pretzels."

The woman instantly put the ribbon-covered plastic headband down on the counter, murmuring, "Thank you."

Destiny gave her a sweet smile. "No problem." The woman headed straight for the door.

Destiny's smile was now genuine as she called after the fleeing customer, "Come back again. We get new stuff all the time."

Sam tried hard not to look amused.

He watched as Destiny crossed and uncrossed her legs a few times, swinging her perfectly shaped calves up into the air and then down again. She finally stopped swishing her limbs and pulled a package of Dutch coffee candy from a display and tore into the sparkling gold bag.

She held out the treats to Sam, who murmured, "No, thank you."

Destiny frowned. "They're good. Little coffee candies. Bitzie—she's the owner—buys them at Costco and then puts 'em in these fancy little bags so people think they got flown over special from somewhere. Go on, try one."

Sam was certain that Riddle would love to get his hands on a coffee candy. But he still shook his head no, adding, "I just ate."

Destiny gave him a penetrating look. "Liar. I can tell, you know."

Sam knew his face was turning red.

She continued. "I hate liars."

Sam felt the need to defend himself. But before he could figure out what to say, Destiny cooed, "But I'll get over it. You see, Sam, I'm looking for a new friend. And you're going to do just fine."

8

Emily watched as the ketchup from the top bottle moved very, very slowly into the bottle she'd positioned below. Maybe, she decided, it wasn't moving at all.

But it had to be. She'd done well in physics. Things shifted, and you couldn't even tell.

At the restaurant, refilling the condiments was part of the job at the end of every shift. The tedious process gave time for her mind to wander back to Sam.

Sam loved ketchup.

It was one of the few things he could get for free at fast-food places. And so he and Riddle would stuff their pockets with the packets. As little kids, if they got hungry late at night, they'd eat ketchup. Just plain. It was probably torture, but somehow that now sounded romantic.

Being in love, she was fully starting to realize, was some kind of all-consuming, full-body reaction. She wanted to do only two things:

Keep it all private and locked inside.

And tell everyone in the world.

The conflicting emotions, she thought, were driving her crazy.

When she wasn't with Sam, she was almost always thinking about being with him. And when she was with Sam, she found herself getting anxious about when they would have to part.

Emily looked at the slow-moving red sludge and decided that she now loved ketchup in some profound kind of way.

What she didn't love was the fact that Bobby Ellis now worked at Ferdinand's. And that he was calling himself Robb.

Her eyes moved across the restaurant, where she could see Leo Saar, the restaurant owner, talking to him.

She and Bobby had the exact same schedule. It was really awkward. They were together from ten thirty in the morning until nine at night or later, with only a one-hour break in between.

Leo had taken Robb aside on the first day and explained things, like how the wine cellar was organized and what was in the artichoke sauce. Robb Ellis fit in right away, which was a complete surprise.

Maybe that was the problem. But the really irritating part was that he seemed to speak the same language as the diners, which wasn't French, but rather the intricacies of "fancy food."

She had to admit, Bobby turned out to be just one of those people who was better after a defeat than a victory.

She wished that she could be more like that. Because she wasn't dealing with the aftermath of the freezer incident very well.

She knew that the dishwashers were joking when they called her the Ice Queen. It was supposed to be funny when the chef put a plastic tub on his head whenever he saw her.

She was certain this was all "workplace humor." That's what her friend Nora had said, and she had more paid job experience. But instead of laughing, Emily found that the whole restaurant now made her tense.

She had imagined that this summer was going to be the most carefree time of her life.

She had it all, she thought.

Didn't she?

*   *   *

Moments after her last ketchup bottle was topped off, Emily and Robb Ellis walked out onto the sidewalk to find Sam talking to a very short girl in a pink skirt inside the Orange Tree gift shop.

Robb noticed them first. "Looks like your boyfriend met somebody."

Emily turned her head to see Sam and the girl.

Sam was standing by the door. He had his hands in his pockets and was listening.

The girl, as animated as if she were performing onstage,

was in the middle of some kind of story. Her arms were moving through the air, and she was laughing.

And while Emily could only see Sam's back, she could tell that he was laughing, too.

Emily headed down the sidewalk to the shop, forcing herself to move at regular speed. Robb Ellis followed. She didn't say anything until she was right behind Sam, and then Destiny Verbeck beat her to the punch.

"Sam—your girlfriend's off work!"

Sam spun around and saw Emily and Robb, both standing in their Ferdinand's Fine French Restaurant attire. Emily thought Sam looked very uncomfortable as he said, "Hey."

He leaned over to kiss her, which was something he wouldn't normally do with Robb Ellis and a stranger standing right there. Emily looked at him. His face was red. Just slightly. Was he blushing? And then Sam started to speak, but before he could, Destiny chirped: "I'm Destiny. Destiny Verbeck. I've heard so much about you, Emily."

But Destiny's eyes floated right past Emily to Robb.

"And you're...?"

Robb Ellis managed to say, "I'm Robb. I—"

Destiny's head tilted back, and she laughed like she'd just heard a joke. A good one. "You work at Ferdinand's, too. I know who you are. Believe me, there's nothing to do in this shop but spy on the world. You drive a new black BMW SUV, and you get your hair done at the Hair Asylum."

Robb couldn't stop himself. "I don't get it done. They wash it. I had a broken arm and—"

Destiny didn't let him finish. "Well, I need to get my hair fixed. Look at my roots. It's so much work being a blond. But the world is nicer to you—so that's a trade-off." Destiny leaned closer to Robb. "I bet by the end of the summer you have all kinds of natural streaks in your hair—right?"

Robb didn't answer. Everyone was silent except for Destiny, who took only a moment before she happily continued.

"I've been too busy to do anything since I got here. The second day I was in town, this job opened up. And the woman who runs the store is sort of a slave driver."

It felt to Emily as if Robb Ellis was falling under some kind of spell as Destiny spoke. He suddenly couldn't take his eyes off her. She heard him say, "Are you going to college here?"

Destiny smiled. Not big but sweet. Like she was flattered at the idea. "Nope. I quit school. Or maybe school quit me. Something happened between us, because it's over. Do you go there?"

Robb volunteered. "We're in high school. At least she and I are." He motioned toward Emily.

Destiny looked at Sam. "What about you, Samuel?"

Emily felt herself bristle. No one called him that. It was too formal. And too intimate for someone who just met him. "He's going to summer school at the college," Emily found herself answering for him. "He already started."

Right away she felt bad. She was being possessive. Or something worse. She was jealous. But of what?

Destiny nodded. "I know it's a great school. That's what I've heard. I'm impressed."

Sam's voice was low. "Don't be."

Destiny smiled at all three of them. "You guys are my first friends here. I feel so lucky. I really don't know anyone, and now I do. Just like that. Should we go get dinner tonight? A group thing."

Emily was suddenly some kind of spokesperson. "Robb and I have to work the dinner shift tonight. We're only on break."

"Sunday, then." Destiny nodded. "I like that better anyway."

The others exchanged looks. Emily was about to say something, but Destiny started talking again.

"Robb, what's your favorite kind of food? Don't think about it. Just answer."

Robb managed: "I like steak, I guess. And cheese."

Destiny's hands swept excitedly up into the air. It was appealingly graceful. "My favorite food right now is Thai. It's spicy and can be sweet and sour and crunchy all at once. That's what's important—that there's something unexpected behind it—right? I mean, bland is bland is boring—right?" She looked right at Sam.

"I really haven't eaten that much Thai food," he replied.

Destiny's face squeezed up. "C'mon. That's crazy. This is a college town. They have to have great Thai."

Emily couldn't stop herself from volunteering: "There's a Thai restaurant on West Eleventh. It's good."

"Of course you would be the one who would know." Destiny took Emily's arm.

And suddenly Emily was certain that in the future she was going to be eating Thai food with a girl she already wished she'd never met.

9

Clarence had lived his whole life by the simple concept that everything he needed was right in front of him.

It was just a fact.

The tools were present for success.

They might not belong to him, but they were always within his reach.

And now, in a space the size of a storage closet, he was putting his theory to the ultimate test.

Pressure from two civil-rights groups (badgered by the legal interns) resulted in an appointment for Clarence Border to leave incarceration and their overburdened medical clinic and seek expert advice for the problems arising from his amputation.

The appointment meant that he'd be escorted outside the prison compound to the city of Merced, California, to a doctor.

And so Clarence prepared.

Step one.

He traded breakfast to an inmate named Bandit for two plastic sandwich bags.

Clarence hated the guy if for no other reason than this: what kind of person in prison for theft calls himself Bandit?

The failure of imagination disgusted Clarence.

But Bandit was hooked up. He had drugs, shanks, cigarettes, cell phones, alcohol, candy—pretty much you name it, Bandit could get his hands on it.

All Clarence wanted was two clear plastic sandwich bags with zip-lock tops.

They cost him the three cold pancakes that were served six days a week at 5:30 AM. Big deal.

The second thing Clarence needed was right in front of him.

The jail was crawling with vermin.

It didn't matter that the floors were scrubbed with straight ammonia or that the number one health priority was trying to keep communicable diseases in check by sterilizing everything.

Rodents, lice, fleas, maggots, bedbugs, ants, pigeons, bats, beetles, silverfish, wasps, centipedes, lizards, moths, and earwigs were all living behind bars.

And doing very well, thank you very much.

While rats might make a daytime appearance on occasion in the exercise yard, they made the kitchen and the trash area the center of their thriving community.

But the mice were different. Their infestation was an equal-opportunity affair.

Everyone saw mice at night, scurrying along the dark walls, squeezing their way in and out of spaces.

And so on the second night after he'd put his plan in motion, Clarence caught a mouse, snapping its dark gray neck as if he were twisting the cap off a bottle of beer.

As he dropped the dead rodent into the first little bag and sealed it shut, he imagined the family who had twisted his sons' minds.

He then used the second bag as another layer of protection.

Was it in his mind, or did his missing foot now hurt less?

Things were suddenly going his way.

No doubt about that.

10

Emily had no idea why they'd all been talked into going out for Thai food with the firecracker in the miniskirt.

But two days later, it was Sunday and everyone had the night off. Destiny said that she would meet them at the restaurant. Emily and Sam were picking up Bobby Ellis.

Now, as Emily looked at herself in the mirror, she found that her white jeans and her blue T-shirt looked boring. She felt certain that Destiny would show up wearing an exotic costume of some sort.

So Emily went back into her closet and found a fitted yellow sundress and a pair of strappy sandals that she had ignored for so long, there was a spiderweb over the left toe area.

She then put on the necklace that she'd worn the day she met Sam. The little coral beads felt as if they had played a part in the magic of that. Satisfied that she was now making a real effort, she headed out of her room.

In the hallway Emily stopped to stare at the yellow reading cards that her mother had placed for Riddle.

Mirror. Rug. Wall. Painting. Air Vent. Window. Staircase. Banister. Plant.

What she saw was alarming. The mirror said *Rug*. The wall was marked *Window*. The plant said *Staircase*. All the cards had been switched.

Emily found Jared watching television. She picked up the remote and turned off the TV, causing her little brother's head to spin around. "Why did you do that?"

She stared right at him. "You moved Mom's reading cards."

Jared didn't flinch.

"It was a joke."

"Well, it's not funny."

Jared wasn't backing down.

"Maybe not to you, but I was laughing."

Emily found herself suddenly getting angry. Too angry.

"You don't know how hard it is for them! You never put yourself in their position!" Jared's eyes narrowed. He didn't see this side of his sister often.

"Why are you yelling at me? It's not your job to yell at me. That's Mom and Dad's job!"

Jared jumped to his feet and ran into the hallway. But he made a point of trying to get in the last word: "You're too excited about finally having a boyfriend to think about anything but that!"

"What does having Sam as my boyfriend have to do with you moving the reading cards? Nothing! Okay?"

She was yelling again. And suddenly it was so obvious that he was a little kid. He had tears in his eyes as he took off. Seconds later she heard the back door slam shut.

Emily started after him and ran right into Riddle, who was waiting at the end of the hall. She could see that he looked pained as he spoke: "It was a joke. He was just being silly."

Emily searched his face. Not many boys his age used the word *silly*. But Riddle never tried to position something. He just told it the way he saw it.

"Really? He wasn't trying to confuse you?"

"No, he *was* trying to do that. That's what's silly. But I still don't understand the words. So *that's* the joke."

Emily nodded, but she was confused. She had overreacted, that much she understood. And then Riddle added, "Sam's late. He's not a late person. He's an early person. Maybe that made you mad, not the moved words."

The two cats appeared from the kitchen and went straight to Riddle. He leaned down and scooped up both of them. Not many people could carry two cats and make it look easy.

But he did.

Emily watched Riddle go back into the kitchen and take a seat by the window. She wanted to protect him, but right now he didn't look like someone who needed it.

Outside she heard Jared bouncing his basketball. She knew she should go say that she was sorry for yelling, but then she heard Sam's car (which was really her car, but he now drove it) pull into the driveway. She was glad her parents weren't home to have witnessed the outburst.

Maybe Jared was right.

Maybe she was too excited about having a boyfriend to think about anything else.

*   *   *

Sam was late because he'd taken a shower at his apartment. His hair was still wet. Emily noticed right away that he was on edge.

"Are you okay?"

He only nodded, keeping his eyes behind him as he reversed down the driveway.

"I don't know how we ended up doing this," Emily added. "The last person I want to have dinner with is Robb Ellis."

She glanced over at Sam and realized that he was clean-shaven.

He only did that every three or four days. Sam answered with: "Let's get this over with as fast as we can."

Emily reached over and took his hand. "Agreed. The whole thing should take an hour, tops. Right?"

Minutes later, when Robb Ellis got in the car, it was obvious that he was wearing a new shirt. Emily knew because the fabric still had the fold lines from the store packaging.

Her eyes drifted down to her sandals. Her toes felt all tight. They were curling and uncurling.

What was going on?

Why were they all suddenly putting in so much effort?

* * *

After driving in awkward silence, the three walked into Thai-Dishes to find Destiny Verbeck already sitting in a booth in the corner. She had a half-empty glass of beer in front of her and jumped up from the red vinyl like she'd been shot from a cannon.

Emily could see that she was wearing a sleeveless pink top that was made of flannel, with a pattern of sleeping teddy bears. She had on matching pink shorts. On her feet were funny little orange high-heeled boots.

Emily had to admit to herself that the girl looked incredibly cute.

Destiny broke the ice by giving each of them a tight hug, pulling Emily closest and whispering into her ear:

"I'm in love with your necklace. It's a-mazing."

Her exuberance, Emily realized, had a way of making them all feel more at ease. Or maybe it was something about her energy level that was distracting.

Destiny next struck a pose as if she were a store manne-quin. She put her hands on her hips, turned to the side, and pushed her pelvis forward.

"Just so you all know, I'm wearing pajamas."

All eyes were now on Destiny's snug, pink flannel outfit.

"I buy most of my stuff in the children's department. And they had these totally cute pajamas, and I couldn't resist. I bought three pairs. Different colors, of course. Once I love something, I just want as much of it as I can get."

67

Robb Ellis stared at the pajama top for what felt to Emily like way too long. Sam, she noticed, kept his eyes focused on a spot on the floor.

Interesting.

Destiny slid back into the booth and took a deep swallow of beer. It was as if she hadn't seen liquid in days. "I started drinking without you guys! Now you have to play catch-up."

Robb Ellis eyed the now empty glass, lowering his voice. "I've got my fake ID."

Sam and Emily exchanged a look as a waiter appeared. "Can I get you started with something?"

Robb tilted his head toward Destiny. "I'll have what she's having."

Emily looked up at the waiter, feeling guilty even though she hadn't done anything. "I'm good with water."

Destiny piped up, "And I need another Singha. Thai beer is amazing. Don't you guys want to try one?"

"I'm driving," Sam responded, but Emily stayed silent. "We're both good with water," he said, and put his arm around Emily as the waiter left the table.

Destiny leaned forward as if she were a detective. "So how'd you two meet?"

Sam stared down at the menu. Emily was confused. Why was he being rude? "At church," she answered.

Destiny looked surprised. "You're both from religious families?"

"No," Sam responded, and his voice now sounded harsh. "And I didn't grow up here." He pulled his arm back, and his body language seemed to suggest that he was in full defensive retreat.

But none of that deterred Destiny, because she flashed him an easy grin. "So, Sam, you're a newbie to this place—just like me!"

Sam looked back down at the menu, but under the table he took Emily's hand. She could feel tension in his grip. Why was he letting this girl bother him?

And then Emily had to ask herself why the word *newbie* was so irritating to her. And why suddenly everything happening at the table seemed to matter so much.

*   *   *

Destiny did most of the ordering, because she appeared to be some kind of food expert. She said that she'd eaten in Thai restaurants all over the country and pronounced the names of the dishes in a way that made the waiter smile.

But it turned out that she liked really *spicy* Thai food, and that meant she needed a lot of beer to wash it all down.

None of that kept her from conducting the meal as if she were a radio talk show host and her three companions were calling in to seek advice. Except they never asked her for any of it.

The girl in the teddy-bear pajamas explained that gum helped keep you awake when you'd been driving for hours. Cats didn't travel well in trucks. And no one should ever leave home without a roll of quarters.

She was also certain that there was no sight as beautiful as the sunrise in the desert after it had snowed. And that it was essential to wear sunscreen even if you were driving all day.

Destiny finally stopped her monologue to heap her plate with a second serving of green curry. She then flagged down the waiter, ordered her fifth beer, and wiggled her way out of the booth. "I'm gonna take a leak."

The other three watched silently as Destiny, not moving in exactly a straight line, made her way to the back of the restaurant. Pretty much everyone in the place was eyeing her at this point, which only made Destiny add a strut to her swagger.

"She's completely wasted," Robb Ellis said, once she was behind the door of the restroom.

Sam nodded. "Smashed."

Emily had to agree. "We should have stopped her."

Robb tentatively took a bite of the green curry. He had barely touched his meal. "She doesn't seem like the kind of person you tell what to do. And I know this is off topic—but this is the hottest food I've ever eaten in my life. My mouth is on fire."

Sam, who up until that moment hadn't thought much of Robb, found himself agreeing. "It's pretty spicy."

Robb started to laugh. "It's possible I now have a hole in my tongue."

Emily could feel herself relax. She looked at the two boys. "What are we even doing here?"

They both shrugged.

And then Emily decided that maybe Destiny intervening in their lives was a good thing.

Sam and Robb/Bobby were now talking, and the stiff weirdness between all of them had simply disappeared.

Because they were now on one side, and Destiny was on the other. And nothing united a group like a common enemy.

* * *

She had been gone a long time. Too long.

Emily knew that something was wrong. She had a way of getting inside a person, even when she didn't want to. And now she had a feeling that Destiny needed her help.

"I better go check on her."

Sam reached for Emily. "Em—I'm sure she's fine. Give her some time to sober up in there."

But Emily was already out of the booth and moving across the room. When she was just outside the bathroom, she heard a loud thud on the other side of the door.

She was too late. By seconds.

Emily entered to find Destiny on the floor. She was bleeding from her forehead and had vomited a massive amount of Thai food. About half of it ended up in the toilet.

The diminutive girl looked up through glassy eyes as she leaned her bloody forehead against the wall and whispered, "It's a good thing I'm wearing pajamas, because I'm ready for bed."

Emily pulled Destiny up onto her feet and led her to the sink. Destiny saw blood gushing from her hairline and gasped. "I'm dying...."

Emily was surprised at how much her voice sounded like her mother's as she said, "You're going to be fine."

Emily lifted the top off a wall dispenser and removed most of what was inside. She then pressed a handful of the brown paper towels against Destiny's wound, all the while keeping her upright.

"The cut's not deep. It's along your scalp. And that area of your body really bleeds."

Destiny took a look at Emily in the mirror. "Are you a nurse? You're a very pretty nurse."

"I'm not a nurse. But my mom is." Emily put the paper towels into Destiny's hand, instructing, "Hold this."

The sight of her own reflection seemed to sober the wobbling girl. She had green-curry puke on one side of her white-blond hair.

"Whoa. I look like a fighter. And I am a fighter. I've had to be a fighter. Because if I wasn't a fighter, I'd be…I don't know what I'd be. But it wouldn't be a fighter. Right? Hey, do you feel that? The room's moving."

Emily couldn't believe that, even in her current state, Destiny was still a chatterbox.

"Try to relax. And breathe deep. Slow inhales and exhales."

Emily repositioned Destiny up against the wall and, with another handful of paper towels, returned to the toilet, where she did her best to mop up the just-puked Thai food.

When she finished, she turned around to find that Destiny had slid down the wall. She was now lying on the green linoleum bathroom floor as if it were a lawn.

Emily was as alarmed at this as at anything else that she had witnessed in the bathroom. "Destiny, get up off that floor!"

Destiny kept her eyes shut. "Do I have to?"

Emily squatted down and pulled the girl up to her feet. "Bathroom floors are gross."

Destiny was as wiggly as a worm. She wasn't vertical for long before she suddenly flopped over, resting her head in the sink.

Emily took the opportunity to turn on the water and wash the vomit out of Destiny's hair.

"Is the water too hot?"

Destiny tried to answer and got a big mouthful of soap. It seemed to sober her up. Her choking then morphed into crying as she pulled her head out of the sink.

"Are you going to leave me?"

Emily looked at the front of Destiny's teddy-bear pajama top. It was soaked. Her cut had stopped bleeding, but her dyed wet hair around the injury was pink. Thick black eyeliner ran down her cheeks, and some of her green eye shadow was in her eyebrows.

Destiny was a sad clown. Her face squeezed up, and she whimpered: "Emmie...don't leave me!"

Emily felt her whole body tense. Since when did somebody call her Emmie? Only her little brother used that name.

But she tried to be reassuring as she took a paper towel and started scrubbing Destiny's face, working hard to get the makeup off.

When she spoke her voice was both compassionate and irritated. "Don't worry. We're going to take you home."

73

The word *home*, however, had a bad effect on Destiny.

Her eyes opened wider, and she flung her arms around Emily's neck and started to sob. Emily tried to comfort her while at the same time pushing her away.

And that's when Destiny's fingers slipped under the coral necklace, snapping it right off.

Emily stared down at the green floor as the petite orange beads scattered. They were no bigger than sesame seeds, and several dozen bounced to the drain centered in the floor, where they then disappeared forever.

Emily tried to stay calm. Her lucky necklace was gone. She was a rational person and didn't believe that the jewelry had some kind of secret power. Just like she knew that losing it wasn't a bad omen.

But then she looked over at weeping Destiny, and suddenly Emily was crying with her.

*　*　*

Sam watched Emily, with an arm around Destiny's waist, lead her back to the table.

He got to his feet, and Robb took the cue and did the same. Robb's alarm made his voice high-pitched. "What happened?"

Destiny was crying but managed: "I broke Emmie's necklace."

"It was an accident. Forget about that now."

Sam met his girlfriend's gaze and realized that she'd been crying as well. What was going on? Suddenly it felt as if all of them were out of control.

Sam helped Destiny back into the booth as Emily explained to the boys, "She fell and hit her head. The necklace broke later."

Destiny's hair was wet. Her lips were pursed up in a pout. Her makeup was mostly gone, and her soaked pajamas now clung like a body stocking.

It was impossible for the boys not to stare.

Before, Destiny was trying hard to look sexy. But now she was vulnerable and exposed, and Sam found himself wanting to pull her close. He couldn't believe that he found the idea of touching the flannel teddy-bear top so appealing.

Sam pushed the idea as far out of his mind as possible, turning away from the table. "I'll get the check."

Robb was at his heels. "Right. I'll go with."

Emily kept Destiny propped up in the booth as Sam and Robb crossed the room to find their waiter. They were both agitated.

As they walked away, Emily could feel something else coming off the two boys.

Desire.

She felt a punch of jealousy hit her gut. She turned back to Destiny, and the girl took her hand, whispering:

"They're both in love with you. How does that feel, Emily?"

*   *   *

Once the bill was settled, Emily and Robb led Destiny, now sandwiched between them, to the car.

Sam went ahead and unlocked the doors. The Bells had bought a third vehicle, and he shared it now with Emily. But mostly it was his, because she walked to work and he had summer school.

That's how good the Bells were. After the thoughts he'd had in the restaurant about Destiny, Sam knew that he didn't deserve any of it.

He put the car in drive and pulled out of the parking lot. Destiny had shut her eyes and was leaning her head out the window like a blond puppy dog that had spent too long at a dog park.

Robb Ellis then stated the obvious: "We've got to get her home."

Emily leaned closer to the boys. "She told me in the bathroom that she doesn't have a home."

Robb glanced in the rearview mirror. "She has to live somewhere."

Destiny lifted her chin up from the window and said: "I keep my things in the basement. In Whitesell." Then she fell back against the door and returned to a stupor.

Robb and Emily knew that Whitesell was one of the large dorm complexes on the college campus. Robb's gaze went from Destiny to Emily. "So she's a college student?"

Sam kept his eyes on the road. "No."

Robb shook his head. "How do you keep your things in a dorm if you're not a student?"

Sam pulled the car to the curb. He turned around and with a firm voice said, "Destiny."

She didn't open her eyes, but she finally answered. "Yeah…"

"You don't have a house or an apartment because you don't have money for rent or to pay for utilities." Destiny appeared to be listening. "And you don't have a car to sleep in. So you just find a place to get through the night—right?"

Destiny's body seemed to tense up.

"Is your mom alive?" Sam continued. Destiny shook her head. "And your father, do you know where he is?"

She seemed to come to life at the question. Her voice now had an edge. "Yeah, and I know where he's going to be for the next ten years. And so does the state of Nevada."

Inside Sam felt a pang of guilt and shame. No wonder someone like Destiny Verbeck had come into his life.

On the sidewalk in front of the restaurant, she'd seen right through him.

They were two of a kind.

11

"It's bedtime, you two." Debbie Bell carried a laundry basket, which she now set down on the couch in the living room. As she began folding clothing, Riddle got up.

"I'll take Felix out for his last sniff of the yard."

Debbie smiled as the boy and dog headed out of the room. Jared scowled. "Riddle should sleep at the apartment. It has two bedrooms."

They'd obviously been over this before. Debbie continued pairing socks. "You know he likes to be with you."

Jared rolled his eyes. "He likes to be with the dog."

His mother lowered her voice. "I'm sure that's part of it, but he feels safe here with us."

Jared never cared about sleeping with Felix until Riddle won the dog's heart. Then it became just one more injustice.

"Felix sleeps on Riddle's bed. Not on the floor."

"I don't want you to worry about that."

Jared dug in. "But Mom, the rule is no dogs on the bed."

Debbie went over and put her arm around her son. "Riddle's still adjusting, sweetheart. You understand that, right?"

Jared squeezed his eyes shut. He wanted to scream to the room that the person adjusting was *him*. He was the one who had to share everything now. His room. His dog. His sister. His mom and dad.

Share. Share. Share.

Was there a worse word in the world? It rhymed with *despair.* That was a grown-up word. Didn't they understand it?

Jared slipped out of his mother's embrace and got to his feet. He wanted to make his footsteps heavy. Like he was pounding his heels into the floor. He tried hard to stomp. And not in a little-kid way. In a way to show he had power in this house, even if he didn't.

The problem was that it was impossible to really stomp when you were thin and had small feet.

So he headed up the stairs and didn't even say good night, because maybe that would make a point.

But as far as he could tell, his mom didn't even notice.

* * *

Minutes later, staring up at the ceiling, wondering if anyone in the house cared that he hadn't used toothpaste when he brushed his teeth, Jared had to admit that his secret wish had always been for a brother.

And somehow he now had two.

79

He was going to be very, very careful in the future about what he wished for. Because no matter what anyone said, Riddle and Sam weren't real brothers, which was what he really wanted.

Riddle was more than two years older than he was. And even though they were the same size, older was older.

Jared knew what was going on. His parents were adopting the kid. They had gone to a lawyer and everything. It was just unbelievable. What were they thinking? Riddle couldn't even read. It was so embarrassing.

Jared had moved the cards that his mother made, because he was trying to make a point. Riddle was too far behind to ever catch up.

And it wasn't just that Riddle was a problem.

Sam wasn't working out that great either.

A really good big brother would want to play games and tell secrets and even be some kind of commander.

He would take the littler kid and make him an apprentice. But Sam didn't do that.

He hung out with Emily all the time.

And when he didn't have his arm around her, Sam was in the basement playing the guitar or listening to music for hours and hours and hours with *Jared's* dad. It was like his father and Sam had a secret clubhouse down there in the studio, and that was just plain creepy.

Plus, for the last few months, his mom and Emily were both really happy all the time, which meant that they really weren't paying attention.

That happens, Jared thought, *to really happy people.*
They don't notice the little things.

*   *   *

Riddle couldn't tell if Jared was asleep.

He'd gone upstairs first, and he had the lights off by the time Riddle got to the room. So Riddle tried to be very quiet as he slipped under the covers. Felix hopped up onto the foot of the bed and circled around three times before flopping down on Riddle's feet.

Riddle then whispered, "Good night, Jared." He didn't get an answer, but that was okay.

Riddle shut his eyes, and in the orange sparkles of darkness he saw letters.

They were everywhere now. Even in front of him before he fell asleep.

The world was full of the symbols, which made confusing sounds. It had been so much easier to just see letters as interesting shapes. The idea that they got together to make up a code was alternately electrifying and horrifying.

If he had been able to read, maybe he could have contacted his mom. Maybe it would have all been different.

Despite how hard it was to make sense of the letters, Riddle went to sleep every night thinking the same thing. Maybe his father would come back for him. Maybe he and Sam weren't really safe.

He didn't tell anyone, but the main reason he wanted to

learn to read was so that he could write a note if he ever was taken again. He wouldn't just draw pictures of things.

He'd use words to find help.

*   *   *

Destiny took small sips from the can of Sprite.

Emily and Sam and Robb Ellis all held cups of coffee. They were sitting now in the parking lot outside Tommy's Market on Seventeenth Street, which was a block from the college.

Once Destiny had gotten all the beer and Thai food out of her stomach, she began to return to the land of the living, or at least the land of the talking, which was the only place she knew.

As Destiny explained it, she'd been on the road for a few years. First with a truck driver. Then on her own. But she'd only been in this town for ten days.

The first thing she did when she arrived was go to the college rec center and take a shower in the women's locker room, using the explanation that she'd left her student ID in her dorm.

From there it wasn't very hard to actually find the housing quad, which she could easily access during the daytime hours. She left her overpacked duffel bag downstairs in the laundry room in a storage closet that no one seemed to use, and she slept on the first floor on the couch in the room designated for dorm meetings.

The very next day, Destiny got a job at the Orange Tree. The owner paid cash.

Destiny didn't know how long she'd stick around. She didn't have much of a life plan. And she also didn't have more than forty-eight dollars to her name.

Sam opened the car door, turning to Robb. "I'm going back into the market to get some gum. You wanna come get some?"

Destiny piped up, "I'll come get gum. My mouth tastes sick."

Sam shot Emily a look, and she reached her hand over to the door handle and kept it there. "You aren't up for walking around a store."

The two boys got out of the car and headed across the parking lot.

Emily glanced over at the clock on the side of the market. It was almost midnight. This was turning into one long dinner. They had to find a way to end it. She wished Robb had stayed with Destiny. Then she and Sam could have come up with a plan.

She knew for a fact that Sam didn't chew gum, so something was going on in there.

Her thoughts were interrupted when Destiny let out a small burp and said, "So what's the story with your boyfriend? Where did he grow up?"

Emily gave what had become her standard answer. "He moved around a lot." But she realized that she sounded defensive, which she was. And she didn't volunteer anything else.

Destiny turned away from the dark glass to look at her. "He's totally hot. That part's no mystery."

* * *

Inside the market Sam seemed a million miles away. Robb didn't want to stare, so he pretended to look at a magazine as he asked: "How much of her story do you believe?"

Sam shrugged. "All of it. Most of it. Enough—put it that way."

Robb thought everyone was always lying, so he was disappointed with the answer. "Even the stuff about driving a big rig?"

"You don't stand five feet tall in heels and pretend that you can operate an eighteen-wheeler."

Robb digested the answer. There was a lot he could learn from this guy. Sam had a certainty about him that was appealing. No wonder Emily liked him so much.

Robb picked up a pack of cinnamon gum from the rack, and the two boys headed to the cash register. Robb dug into his pocket, but Sam had money already out on the counter.

"So what do we do with her?" Robb asked.

Sam sighed. "She's a stray cat. We already fed her. She'll be hard to shake now."

* * *

Destiny said that she lasted only one night at the dorm before the girls called security. Since then, she'd been sleeping in the

84

library, hiding in the fourth-floor bathroom until the building closed down at midnight and then curling up on a soft couch in the reference room until 6:00 AM, when it reopened.

But that hardly seemed like a plan to the rest of the group, and it didn't matter anyway, because the library was now closed.

There was an extra bedroom at Sam's apartment, because Riddle didn't sleep there much.

Emily waited for Sam to bring it up.

But he didn't, and she was so relieved. She wondered to herself if that was wrong. Was it not the charitable thing to do?

And then Robb Ellis came through.

Robb found himself wondering later if that had been Sam's plan all along. Maybe that's why he took him into the store to get the gum. It set him on the course of feeling more responsible.

Robb had the keys to his parents' two-story building downtown, and of course he knew the security code to get in.

There was a comfortable couch in his father's office, and after a quick stop at his house, a sleeping bag became part of the arrangement.

At one in the morning, Destiny, now fairly sober, pressed her head into a pillow on Derrick Ellis's leather sofa. A slow, crooked smile crossed her face as she said, just before she fell asleep, "And I'm already in my pajamas...."

12

Monday was the appointment.

Early.

An armed prison guard named Denny Piercey was his escort.

Clarence called Denny "sir." He made sure to be extra compliant and overly cooperative. He thanked Denny over and over again for his effort.

And when the time was right, Clarence began to cry.

He stared out the window through the wire grate, knowing that the guard could see him in the rearview mirror.

He remembered being a kid in Alaska and how a logging truck had lost its brakes and plowed into the front of David's Candy Shop.

Clarence was eight years old. When he'd walked down Main Street, he saw other kids coming toward him. They were all stuffing their faces with candy.

Little Clarence ran as fast as he could down the hill to the accident, and when he got there, he heard the news. With the front of his store destroyed, David Dewey had given away all his shop's candy.

And Clarence was too late.

He'd missed the biggest freebie in the little town's history.

The incident didn't just put a lump in Clarence's throat; it broke his tiny, already twisted spirit.

And now, dozens of years later, it could still make him weep. Without a sound he managed to get tears to spill from his muddy eyes and tumble down his pale cheeks.

* * *

When they reached the city of Merced, it was even better than he'd imagined.

The area outside the two large medical office buildings was hectic. The parking lot was full, and there was a rack right in front that was packed with bikes.

Clarence did his best to make it seem that he looked at nothing as he was escorted from the van.

But he saw it all.

Once they were inside the medical center, Clarence asked if he could use the bathroom.

The corrections officer looked at Clarence and his tear-stained face, his ill-fitting fake leg, and decided to remove the handcuffs. He didn't want to unzip the guy's pants.

Clarence was over-the-top grateful as he disappeared inside the stall to relieve himself. He did his business quickly and made a point of carefully washing his hands with lots of soap and hot water, not rinsing them completely so that the sweet, clean smell would linger.

Upstairs, with the handcuffs back in place, the two men sat together in the doctor's waiting room.

There was an aquarium lining one wall in the office. As Clarence stared at the brightly colored fish he suddenly saw them being plucked off a tropical reef.

Now they were prisoners.

And like him, the fish had done nothing wrong. Clarence got tears in his eyes for the second time in one day.

But these ones were real.

* * *

When it was his turn to go in, the prisoner spoke softly to the doctor about the phantom pain, about the ill-fitting replacement leg, and in a special touch, he told the physician that his fish in the waiting room were an inspiration—they were so free in their movement.

Clarence had spent hours before the visit rubbing his prosthetic leg back and forth, wearing the skin down to a raw stump. He now behaved like an absolute gentleman, thanking everyone who came within three feet of him.

And all the while, he was taking in the details.

This doctor, the expert, was on the second floor.

And the bathroom for the patients was at the end of the hall.

When the examination was over, Clarence complained about his sour stomach. He was escorted again into the bathroom, and corrections officer Denny Piercey waited on the other side of the stall door.

Clarence undid his prison-issue work pants and silently removed the doubled plastic bag that was tucked deep in his underwear. Inside the bag was the decomposing dead mouse.

Clarence quietly pulled apart the zip-lock and held the bag, now open, against the stall door. On the other side, the prison guard got a sudden whiff of the putrid smell of death.

He stepped back, exhaling. "I'm going to wait outside while you do your business."

Behind the door Clarence smiled. "Sorry about that, sir. I've got all kinds of trouble with my digestion."

Clarence heard the door shut, and in an instant he was out of the stall and the dead mouse was floating in the toilet bowl. The plastic bags was shoved back into his prison underwear as he went to the window.

It was large but covered by a security grate. Clarence removed a dime and two pennies from his left sock. Lady Luck was on his side. The dime fit into the slot of the screws that held the metal bracket that supported the grate.

Moving quickly but not hurrying, because hurrying led to mistakes, Clarence loosened all four screws on the grate.

But he didn't pull it down. He left it there, hanging now by a thread. Literally.

And then he went to the stall, hit the flushing mechanism with his foot, and proceeded to the door.

Clarence smiled as he limped, in real pain, out to the hallway. He had always taken pride in the fact that he had a rattlesnake tattoo swirling down his leg. But his amputation had sliced the reptile in two.

Now his mind only had one thought: they could cut off the tail of a snake, but it could still coil.

13

Destiny's eyes opened Monday morning, and she found herself staring at a golf club. It was leaning against a wood-paneled wall.

She looked around in the dim light and took in the two matching leather club chairs, the solid mahogany desk, and the framed educational degrees next to prints of green-headed ducks.

Where was she?

Destiny pulled her knees to her chest and swung the powder-blue sleeping bag down to the floor as she sat up.

It was all coming back to her now.

The guy Robb had a father. And this was where that man worked.

It was a lot more impressive in the day than at night, after too much beer and a lot of Thai food that she'd seen twice.

Destiny climbed out of the sleeping bag and went to the

desk. It was covered with files and documents. There was so much to check out.

And Destiny loved looking through other people's things.

*   *   *

Sam had trouble sleeping.

He tossed and turned his way to daybreak and then got up, took his guitar, and worked on a series of chord progressions he'd been going over with Emily's dad.

He needed to center himself.

But even two hours of music didn't work to slow his heart, which felt like it was beating too fast.

Something was really wrong, that was for sure.

And so Sam put on his shoes and left the apartment. He stuffed his cell phone in his pocket and headed out the door, but he wasn't going to drive. He'd walk.

Hopefully it would calm him down.

Once outside Sam forced himself to confront the demon that was making him so uneasy.

It was Destiny.

She was trouble.

He couldn't stop thinking about how she'd looked in the soaked pajama top. He could see the outline of her body, and he could feel her gaze as their eyes met.

Sam sucked in a deep breath and walked faster.

And then he made a decision.

He had an ATM card now. And he had money. A valuable penny had been sold at auction months before, and he and Riddle had received the profits. The Bells were watching over the funds, but he had access to the account.

He knew what he had to do. He would take out cash and give it to Destiny Verbeck, and in exchange for that she would agree to leave town.

Sam started toward the bank on Olive Street, wondering what time Destiny showed up at the Orange Tree so that he could get it all done.

Hadn't his father always said that people could be bought and sold? Sam knew what it felt like to have nothing. And Destiny had admitted that she fit into that category.

Knowing that he had a plan made him feel better.

He needed that girl gone.

*　*　*

Robb Ellis set his alarm clock for eight thirty that morning.

It was Monday, but his father had a court appearance and would not be going into his office until after lunch. And his paralegal and his assistant didn't roll in until ten.

This gave Robb more than an hour to get to the building and make sure that Destiny had followed directions.

She was supposed to put the sleeping bag in the storage room at the end of the hall, where all the office supplies were kept, and then exit out the back door without setting the alarm.

All he had to do was drive by and make sure everything

was cool in his dad's office and then set the security system and take off. He'd then swing by Mickey D's and get an Egg McMuffin and a Coke before going to work at the restaurant.

Easy.

But Robb Ellis had nothing like intuition or a sixth sense. Half the time he had no understanding of a situation even when it was laid out right in front of him.

It was kind of amazing that his mother was a detective, because he had to work hard to understand anything about people.

So when he opened the front door to the Law Offices of Ellis and Company, he was genuinely surprised to hear loud music blaring.

Robb felt queasy. This wasn't good.

Moving fast now, he went past the receptionist's desk and down the narrow corridor to his father's office.

No one was there.

But closer inspection revealed that his blue sleeping bag was on the floor, and so were what looked like a pair of pink pajamas. Wasn't Destiny wearing them the last time he saw her?

Robb now realized that on his dad's desk was a small transistor radio. He found the Off button and silenced the pounding beat. And that's when he saw a cardboard box that said *Disaster Preparedness Kit*.

Wasn't that normally in the hall closet?

The box was open, and a wrapper for an energy bar

and two empty water bottles were next to the little battery-powered radio.

Robb's eyes moved around the room as if he were investigating a crime scene—which, he felt certain, was now the case.

He then took a deep breath and turned toward the doorway and found himself slamming straight into Destiny.

She was in a leopard-print bra and little matching panties.

And that's when Robb Ellis screamed.

*　*　*

Emily woke up with a headache. The clock on her bedside table showed that it was almost ten.

How had she slept so late?

Emily pulled herself out of bed and grabbed an extra-large sweatshirt from a chair covered in several layers of previously worn clothing. She slipped on the hoodie and went downstairs.

A note on the counter said that her mom had taken the boys to a goat farm. What was up with that? Then she remembered that Riddle was very interested in goat cheese. But Jared? She couldn't imagine he wanted to go hold a baby goat. The note said that they'd taken Felix with them.

Emily poured herself a cup of cold coffee and took a seat at the kitchen table.

The house was quiet.

That was never the case. Especially lately.

Music, video games, the dog, the two cats, the back door slamming, the churning washing machine, and the sighing dryer were always part of the house's audio track. But now it was as if someone had pulled the plug on the whole operation.

Even though it was warm outside, and the sun poured through to the kitchen table, a shiver ran down Emily's spine.

Something ominous was in the air.

Emily looked down at her feet and watched her toes curl and uncurl.

Then she got up to make them stop, dumped the icy coffee into the sink, and did her best to shake it all off.

*　*　*

Robb Ellis found his Destiny.

And that turned out to be a five-foot girl with white-blond hair who figured that anyone who had a father with an impressive law-school degree, a mother who ran a business in the same building, and a credit card already issued in his own name had something substantial to offer.

So when Destiny kissed Robb that morning and then pinned him down on the leather couch, all he could think was that he was super happy he'd brushed his teeth.

And he wished that he hadn't turned off the pounding dance music on the emergency-preparedness radio.

It would have been the perfect sound track for the morning.

* * *

Sam was waiting for her in the shadows of the doorway next to the entrance of the gift shop.

But he was too late.

When Robb Ellis's SUV pulled up to the Orange Tree, Sam watched as Destiny leaned over and gave Robb a deep, moving kiss, as if he were going off to war and she would think of him every minute of every day until he returned.

Once she was out of the truck and Robb had driven off, Sam emerged without so much as a good morning or a hello.

"We need to talk."

Destiny's enormous eyes focused on Sam. She handed him her Styrofoam cup of coffee and grinned as she pulled out a key from her purse.

"I didn't expect to see *you* here waiting for me! It's my lucky day."

Destiny turned the key in the lock and flipped the sign in the front window to Open. She then skipped to the back of the store and hit the switch for the fans and the lights and pressed Play on the music dock. Destiny moved to the beat as a boy band started to sing.

By the time Destiny got to the counter, Sam had his wallet out and handed her five bills. All one hundreds.

"I'm going to pay for your relocation. Tell your boss an out-of-town emergency came up and take off tonight. There's bus service. Or the train."

He wasn't looking at her. But she was staring at him.

She reached across the counter and pushed the bills back at him. "Put your money away. I'm not going anywhere. This place is home now."

Sam finally met her gaze. "I can give you more. I have an ATM card."

But Destiny turned her back on him and pulled a tube of pink, shiny lip gloss from her bag. In one swirl her lips were glistening like candy.

"Don't be crazy. I just told you, I'm staying. There are all kinds of possibilities for me in this town."

When she swung back around, she was looking at Sam in a new way. It was like she was hungry and he was a plate of buttermilk pancakes. "Why do you want to get rid of me so bad?"

Sam could feel his face grow hot. "You're trouble. I don't need it."

Destiny stood up straighter, making her chest stick out and her flat-flat stomach recede into a curve. "Really? Trouble for who?"

Sam put the money back in his pocket and started for the door. "You're leaving. It's just a matter of when."

He heard Destiny as he headed off down the sidewalk.

And she was laughing at him.

14

It rained Monday night.

That didn't happen much in the summer.

One minute the sky was a star field, and the next a warm shower was falling from above.

Emily and Sam were lying on the grass on a blanket out back behind Sam's apartment, and when the sky opened up, they ran for cover.

Now they were on the old couch that was under the awning at the building's entrance.

Sam's arms held her close, and Emily felt completely connected to the most interesting person she'd ever known.

He had spent years living on the road, held hostage by his unhinged father, and he now appreciated everything in a way that made the simplest events seem magical.

They were there for each other. They were meant to be together.

And they would be.

Always.

Emily inhaled and smelled soap and some kind of salty sweetness that was always present on his neck. The stubble of his beard was rough against her face. She felt foolish that she had worried about a meaningless girl in a gift shop. The outside world was no threat to what they had.

Emily kissed Sam, and the force of what she felt took her breath away.

So moments later it was as if icy water had managed to fall straight through the awning when he said:

"I think Robb is with Destiny."

Did she hear him correctly? Was he talking about Robb Ellis and the drunken girl from the Thai restaurant who she hoped no one ever saw again?

"What do you mean—'with' her?"

Sam's voice was even:

"With her. Like together as a couple."

So that's what was on his mind.

She and Sam were together in each other's arms, and that's what was in his head?

She struggled to sound as calm as possible. "Really? Why do you think that?"

Sam's voice was unemotional. "I saw them together."

"Where?"

Sam was matter-of-fact. "In front of the Orange Tree."

Emily let this sink in. She didn't work this past Monday at the restaurant. She didn't need to be picked up.

So why was Sam in front of the Orange Tree?

She realized, now, that she hadn't heard much about his day. He had a tutor and, of course, he always played his guitar for at least two hours. But she'd been at his apartment since after lunch. Why was he just now bringing this up?

But instead of asking that, she simply said: "Oh."

And then she was silent.

Her "oh" hung in the air, and she saw it like a letter in the alphabet, not an expression.

O.

At some point in the day, Sam had gone to the Orange Tree.

O. O. O.

What did that mean? She focused on the letter.

O

O

O

The shape was appearing in her mind now like a zero. It was a circle. It was complete.

And then Sam said: "I went to talk to her. That's when I saw them."

Emily felt her left eyebrow arch. Involuntarily.

He went to talk to her?

Did he just say that?

O. O. O.

Yes, that's what he'd said.

Emily opened her mouth but didn't say *Oh.* Instead, with an even voice, she found herself asking: "Why did you want to talk to her?"

Sam didn't look at her, but he also didn't make it sound like a big deal.

"I wanted to tell her to leave town. I tried to give her money to do that. I know the kind of person she is. She would have taken it, but Robb Ellis got in the way."

Emily opened her mouth again and in a whisper said: "Oh."

This time when she said the word it was:

Ohhhhhh.

The *h*'s had appeared.

The *oh* had two syllables.

There was disclosure happening.

And this news was now all a surprise to her.

* * *

He was honest about things.

The boy raised by the born liar was the truth teller.

Sam proceeded to explain to Emily that Destiny would use people. He could see it. She would take things. She would cause damage.

And now she was conning Robb Ellis.

He had known something like that was coming.

But what he didn't say was that Destiny was also some kind of emotional magnet, and that he felt her pull. He didn't say that her body was full and bursting out of her clothing and available to him.

No.

He didn't say that.

He was honest, but he wasn't able to fully admit that to himself, much less to Emily.

He didn't have to.

Because she knew.

* * *

Emily gave Sam a quick kiss good-bye in the car. Her car.

She hoped that she gave the appearance that nothing was wrong.

Because nothing was wrong.

Right?

Wrong.

Sam and Emily. Emily and Sam. This moment. Forever.

She couldn't take a picture of them as a couple and put that image in a frame and call it done. As in, this is it. The two of us.

Pure joy and true love and even ecstasy were like all things in this world. They had limits.

And borders.

Sam Border.

One moment he could give her his heart and she could possess it completely, but what she had to hope for was that he moved in the same direction she did.

She had to believe that if someone else crossed his field of vision and grabbed his attention that it was fleeting.

Just a distraction.

But now this.

The girl named Destiny had more in common with Sam than she did. They had fathers in prison. Mothers who were gone. They had lived on the edge of something.

Did that mean they understood each other in a way she never would? Did it mean that he felt drawn to her?

Emily saw the way Destiny looked at Sam. She was attuned to people's emotions enough to know exactly what was behind that.

And she also saw some kind of understanding in his eyes when he looked at that strange girl.

She could see that he was afraid.

Not of Destiny.

But of himself.

15

Emily double-clicked the computer in the restaurant kitchen. It recorded the time you arrived for work and sent an e-mail.

She grabbed one of the black aprons from the clean stack in the supply closet, tied it around her waist, and forced herself to be in the moment.

She needed to be here at Ferdinand's, not thinking about Sam or Robb or Destiny. Certainly *not* about Destiny.

Emily went through the door to the back alley to get the rolling plastic trash bin that was used for recycling the wine bottles. It sometimes got left outside.

And there, pressed up against the brick wall of the old building (their clothed bodies intertwined like the two mating pythons she had seen in a documentary on the Discovery Channel), were Robb Ellis and Destiny.

And Destiny was now wearing the workers' uniform of Ferdinand's Fine French Restaurant.

* * *

When Robb Ellis called and said that he had the perfect new employee, someone who could work the floor or help in the office with the accounting, Leo said to bring her in.

The owner had seen right away that the young woman was a fireball of enthusiasm, and he'd hired her on the spot. So what if they now had too many service people? Leo would just let someone go.

Maybe Emily Bell, who had locked herself in the freezer and cut down the expensive insulated door curtain. It wasn't her fault, but he couldn't help but blame her.

Business was down this month, and that ambulance out front hadn't done anything to help. He couldn't stop himself from wanting her out of his sight.

And so now, Wednesday morning, he assigned Emily to train Destiny Verbeck. The larger plan was taking shape. He'd get the new girl to replace the one with the bad luck.

* * *

Emily didn't know anything about Leo's employment plan. She only knew that Sam was right: Robb Ellis and Destiny were together.

They came in from the alley soon after Emily found them. Robb had a streak of sparkling pink lip gloss on his upper lip. Emily thought about telling him but decided not to, which was unlike her.

Instead she took in the fact that the uniform's black

wraparound skirt that was supposed to hit at the knees touched Destiny's ankles. And somehow, that seemed sexier than the way the other girls wore the garment.

The same was true of the restaurant's custom top. Emily fit into hers, but on Destiny, the blouse slipped off her shoulders, looking strangely French. And because it was too long, she knotted it at the waist.

It was now, Emily thought, like some kind of exotic costume.

Destiny wore a rope of green glass beads around her neck and matching green glass miniature-wine-bottle earrings. There was real liquid inside that you could see if the light was shining just right. Emily noticed right away, but Destiny pointed out the bobbles in case she hadn't.

Destiny had found a black satin ribbon that had been left behind from someone's birthday celebration, and she tied it around her head to keep her platinum straw hair out of her eyes.

It made her look like an adorable present.

Emily wanted to run right out the door. But instead she tried her hardest to smile as she said, "I guess you're going to be shadowing me. Well, working as a bus girl is a lot more complicated than it looks."

Destiny nodded. "Tell me about it! One of the places where I waitressed served this flaming duck in orange sauce, and we all had to cook the last part by pouring brandy over the thing. Right at the table! Can you believe that? I almost caught a few customers on fire!"

Emily found herself swallowing hard. "So you've worked in a restaurant before?"

Destiny tugged on her shirt, exposing more of her left shoulder. "Oh, yeah. Coffee shops. I was a waitress in a sushi place and learned how to make the California rolls. That was crazy. And I worked at a chop house, and they let me cut up the meat, but I was too small to really carry the carcasses, so I got replaced."

Emily was hoping that her wide smile didn't look too fake. "Wow. That's great. So you pretty much know your way around a kitchen?"

Destiny tilted her head to the side and her oversize eyes widened. "Well, I don't know my way around *this* kitchen. Show me, Emmie!"

* * *

As it turned out, Destiny pointed out to Emily that the heating drawer with the bread had the temperature set too high, and that was why the rolls were always drying out.

Destiny wrapped folded napkins around the handles of all the metal water pitchers to stop the constant dripping from the condensation.

She fixed the hinge that stuck on the swinging door going out into the dining room by shoving in the pin at an angle.

And an hour later, when a skillet of grease burst into flames and neither of the chefs could find the lid, Destiny picked up a box of salt and put out the fire in an instant.

Emily was in awe.

And all that was before a lunch customer named Michael Schwartz, who was seated at table eight, got a lima bean stuck in his throat. His dining companion jumped to her feet after he suddenly, midsentence, stopped breathing.

The diner silently flapped his thick arms like a huge bird as his face began to turn blue. People around the dining room began shouting about the Heimlich maneuver.

Emily was frozen by the kitchen door, but Destiny sprinted across the room and slammed Michael Schwartz's back with the heel of her small hand. She did it so hard that it looked like an assault.

Destiny whacked the man five times and then, on the sixth hit, the lima bean shot right out of the guy's open mouth onto his plate and bounced into his water glass.

There were cheers from the other diners as the large customer began gasping for air, but Destiny didn't acknowledge them and ran straight into the kitchen.

Emily found her crying in the stockroom. Destiny explained that her own mother had died by choking, and no one had been there to save her. She didn't add that there had been an overdose involved.

After that Emily asked to go home early for the day. She'd had enough. It did not go unnoticed to her that the owner looked thrilled to get her off the clock.

How could she feel anything but sympathy for someone whose mother had died? Especially in such a tragic way?

And how could she feel superior to a girl who was better on her first day at every aspect of work in the restaurant than she was?

Destiny was not what she appeared to be.

And nothing was more unsettling.

16

Things were changing for Clarence Border.

It was now Wednesday, and on Monday the doctor with the hairy arms and the thick eyebrows was going to see him again for a battery of new nerve testing. And Clarence was determined to make that trip outside of prison very worthwhile.

It all revolved around his leg.

Whenever he could, Clarence now took off his artificial limb and leaned it against the toilet, which, like nearly every toilet inside the prison, was made entirely of stainless steel.

All the plumbing was behind the wall, leaving no parts that could be broken off in a fit of rage or scavenged in order to make weapons. There wasn't even a proper seat. Or a handle.

The average person in America flushes a toilet eight times a day, but the average inmate flushes the toilet thirty times a day. This is because a prisoner uses the toilet as an ashtray, a garbage pail, and even a place to cool down soda cans. And Clarence often used the metal bowl to cool down his fiery stump.

He got up off the cot and lifted his leg into the water. He was about to press the metal button on the wall to flush when he saw his future in his peripheral vision: a mud-colored mouse moving along the far wall.

Clarence kept his stump in the toilet bowl, and with lightning speed lifted his artificial leg, bringing it straight down on the rodent. The mouse's skull flattened on impact.

It was truly Clarence's lucky day.

He grabbed the bloodied mess and put it into the zip-lock plastic bag that only days earlier had held the mouse's decomposing third cousin. And now this little rodent would have plenty of time to rot before the doctor's appointment.

Clarence suddenly realized that he was smiling.

Because his side was now winning.

*　*　*

Riddle didn't want anyone to realize that there were mice in the Bells' kitchen.

So he cleaned up after them.

He was certain that if the Bells knew, traps would be set and the killing would begin. He was counting on the little rodents smelling the two cats and deciding to move on without intervention.

But it had been days now, and the little droppings were

still there each night under the kitchen sink. Without his new glasses, he never would have seen.

He couldn't stop himself from feeling sorry for them. The few times he'd caught a glimpse of the tiny creatures, they were running. And they looked terrorized.

He knew the feeling.

And so he waited until the house was quiet and everyone was asleep before he went down to the kitchen.

There was something that happened when he was standing by the sink that brought him back to his old life. Maybe it was that the world was in shadow.

Was it the darkness?

As he cleaned up the little pellets with a paper towel, he suddenly felt his father. It was as if he were there.

Riddle knew that Clarence was in prison, but would the day come when the man would return?

Would he and his brother end up back in a truck?

*   *   *

Riddle could hear Jared's thick breathing. He didn't stir when Riddle came into the room, and neither did Felix. He wasn't much of a watchdog once the sun went down.

There was a full moon out, and the bluish light coming in the window made Jared's action figures seem larger.

Jared claimed he never played with the plastic superheroes anymore, but Riddle had seen him carrying them around and whispering as if they were real.

Jared knows how to work the television
And all of the electrical things in the house.
But he's never had a brother
Only a sister
And that's different.
I will look out for him
The way Sam watched out for me.
Jared needs me, but he doesn't know that.
I need everyone in this house.
Even the mice under the sink need
Someone to be there for them.

*   *   *

Debbie Bell thought that Jared and Riddle should have summer jobs to make pocket money.

And that was why she was pleased when the next-door neighbors asked for help taking care of their house while they were gone for two weeks.

Normally, Emily would have taken this assignment, which consisted of bringing in their mail, watering the houseplants, and feeding the fish in the Binghams' saltwater aquarium.

But Emily was working at the restaurant, and her life was too busy to add anything else. So Riddle and Jared got the job.

The two boys went over to the neighbors' house the following afternoon.

They both listened, but it was Riddle who really paid

attention when Bertie Bingham showed them the weird flakes that the big-eyed fish ate and how much to water the indoor rubber tree plant.

Walking back home across the yard, Riddle said that instead of splitting the money, Jared could keep what the Binghams were going to pay. Riddle couldn't read the spidery handwriting on the to-do list, and he had a bad feeling about being responsible.

Jared wondered if it was some kind of trick.

But Riddle didn't try to manipulate things. That was part of what made him so strange. He didn't whine or complain or say something was unfair.

As far as Jared was concerned, it was unfair that Riddle didn't say when life was unfair.

It made Riddle some kind of ninja or something.

17

The day had come to begin settling the score.

Clarence shoved the zip-lock bag with the second decomposed mouse into the most private part of his underwear.

He put a fresh piece of gum in his mouth. It was his last trade with Bandit. He'd handed over his toothbrush for a single stick.

He now waited patiently for the guard to escort him through security and was thrilled to see that it was once again Denny Piercey who was to take him to the medical appointment in Merced.

Clarence was even more polite and appreciative this time as they boarded the windowless van and headed out of the prison complex. He told Piercey that he was hopeful that these new tests would help find a solution to his nerve problems.

The guard, not much of a talker, admitted that he had a health problem himself. A frozen shoulder.

Clarence suggested that Piercey speak to the doctor about it in Merced. He was, after all, a nerve-and-joint expert.

Piercey shrugged, but inside he thought to himself that maybe he would just get a little free medical advice.

Yup, he might just do that.

*　*　*

It was getting close to the lunch hour when Clarence and Piercey took their seats in the doctor's waiting room.

Clarence wore a pair of orange scrubs. The medical clothing company that provided uniforms to many of the workers in the building had recently added a new line of bright outfits.

And so Clarence had his first piece of good luck for the day.

He looked like a medical professional, not a convicted thief and child abductor. And because he was tall and lean and good-looking, people glanced with more suspicion at the chunky prison guard in his harsh uniform than at him.

"Book and cover" lesson, Clarence thought, *let's hear it one more time.*

As Clarence and Piercey had traveled to Merced, Clarence made a point of saying that his stomach hurt.

And then once they had arrived, after they had checked in and were five minutes into the wait, Clarence turned apologetically to Piercey.

"I'm so sorry, man, but I gotta use the bathroom before we go in there."

Piercey exhaled with irritation but got to his feet and went to the receptionist. "He needs to use the toilet. We'll be right back."

They both already knew the procedure for the restroom key, which was attached to a plastic coat hanger so you couldn't possibly stick it in your pocket and forget.

Once they were walking, Clarence went to work manipulating his right hand in his pants pocket to get hold of the bag with the mouse.

Right before they arrived at the men's room door, just in time to make a difference, he got the zip-lock cracked open. The stench was immediate.

Piercey got a whiff and stood back. "I'll wait out here."

Clarence nodded. The look on his face said that he was deeply grateful. "Sorry, man. I'll try to make it fast, but it's not something I can control."

Clarence disappeared into the bathroom, and the door swung shut. Piercey, still holding a celebrity gossip magazine from the reception area, leaned against the wall to wait.

Once behind the door, Clarence cupped his hand and spit out his chewing gum. He held the knob still and pushed the gum straight into the lock.

Done.

He next threw the decaying mouse in the trash can and placed the remaining bag right up against the threshold.

Clarence then silently, swiftly lifted the already loosened grate off the window. It was easier than he'd anticipated, and in a matter of seconds, the metal shield was resting on the floor.

Clarence propped the grate in front of the door. He then turned on the cold water in the sink, grabbed a handful of paper towels from the dispenser, and stuffed them into his pants pocket.

Despite the fact that Clarence had an artificial leg, there was nothing clumsy about his movements. He swiftly made his way out the window and down the metal ladder of the fire escape.

When he reached the last rung, he jumped eight feet to the ground, landing so that his good leg took the compression of the fall.

There were people on the sidewalks and in the parking lot, but since he was dressed in what looked like medical clothing, moving in such a casual and confident way, no one saw him as suspicious.

Clarence made his way to a bike rack. With the exception of women's purses, he had probably stolen more bicycles than any other single item in his long history of sticky fingers.

Normally he had tools, which allowed him to snap a lock in one swift maneuver. But today was still a breeze.

The bike rack in the front of the medical complex had several dozen bikes waiting for him at odd angles. One was improperly locked to the steel stand.

And one was all it ever took.

Clarence smiled and said hello to a woman passing by, another violation of criminal behavior, where the unwritten code says, "Never make eye contact with anyone."

With the paper towels from the bathroom in hand, he

made it appear that he was wiping off the bike. What he really did was pop a tire from one bike and switch it out onto a second bike.

In under a minute, he was good to go.

He could have been part of a race team. Tire off and on. Lock dropped. Vehicle back on the track.

He did an invisible high five to the rest of his imaginary pit crew as he pedaled away.

18

Sam got a text from Emily. Apparently Destiny was now an employee at the restaurant.

He couldn't believe it. The last thing he needed was for the impossibly hot girl to become friends with Emily.

But whether or not they were friends, he felt certain that Destiny was going to cause problems in his relationship with Emily.

Maybe she already had.

Nothing got past Emily. The issue wasn't that she was perceptive. She was more than that. She didn't just understand him; she could feel what he was feeling.

And that was scary.

It meant that Emily could look at him and know if he was off balance. And if she hadn't already sensed it, she would soon figure it out.

Sam slipped his cell phone back into his pocket and made a new plan for the day.

This morning was the tour of the college library for incoming students in the fall. But today he couldn't bear to pretend to be just an average college student.

He didn't deserve someone like Emily. He didn't deserve her good family and all their kindness. Why did they trust him when he didn't even trust himself?

He was the son of a crook and a thief, and no amount of pretending was going to change that.

It wasn't that Destiny Verbeck was trouble.

He was.

*   *   *

Destiny didn't bother to let the lady who owned the Orange Tree know that she wasn't coming in because she'd taken another job.

She didn't even think about it until after lunch service, when she was sitting in the back helping Justin, the head-waiter, add up the tips.

What if Bitzie Evans, who ran the store, was friends with Leo, who owned the restaurant, and what if she started talking trash about her? Suddenly Destiny realized that she should have said something.

She smiled at Justin, who was trying to figure out why all the figures didn't add up. "I'll be right back."

Justin barely looked in her direction.

Destiny headed for the alley door, and Justin called after her, "You shouldn't smoke out there. Leo doesn't allow it."

"I'm just getting some air. I'll be back in five."

And before Justin could take his questioning any further, the door swung shut.

* * *

Destiny headed straight down the narrow service alley to the sidewalk.

Once on the street, she could see the open door to the gift shop. Bitzie Evans was inside, and she was standing with her hands on her hips and her chest all puffed out.

And then Destiny realized that Bitzie was talking to someone in the shadows. He was tall. Dark hair. His head angled in a different direction, and Destiny recognized him.

It was Sam.

What was he doing in there?

Destiny's stomach did a small flip-flop. But she'd learned to meet her challenges head-on. And so she marched right into the gift shop.

When Destiny entered, Bitzie Evans looked over and said, "Well, well, well, look what the cat drug in. We were just talking about you."

Sam turned to the door and saw Destiny, and for a second his face flashed something she took to be guilt.

"So you have a job at the restaurant?" Bitzie continued. "That's what your friend Sam here was just telling me."

Destiny looked from Bitzie to Sam.

"And Sam says that he's found me a replacement, which I appreciate."

Destiny still didn't say anything, which was unusual for her.

Bitzie filled the dead-air space. "He said they were short-handed over at Ferdinand's and you jumped at the opportunity, which I guess I understand. I wish that you'd called, but considering another girl's been found to replace you, I can't be that mad—right?"

Destiny smiled. It wasn't her sexy smile; it was her chipper, toothier "I'm on your side" smile.

Sam didn't take his eyes off the owner, but he moved several steps toward the door. "I gotta go. Nice to meet you, Mrs. Evans."

"It's Bitzie. Call me Bitzie. It's a nickname. Bite-size."

And then, even though Bitzie Evans was thirty-five years old and had a muffin-top waist that spilled over her pants, she added, "And there's no *Mr. Evans* at this point."

The shopkeeper laughed, and Destiny felt her shoulders literally sink an inch with relief. The high-strung woman was obviously all about Sam now. Destiny could have been invisible.

So Destiny turned to Sam and said, "Let's go."

Once Sam was outside, he started moving fast. Destiny scurried after him. "Hey, can I talk to you?"

He didn't answer.

"So you want Emmie to quit the restaurant? Because I'm working there? And so you went to see if she could have my old job?"

He kept walking. Destiny took off at a run and got ahead of him, turning around to face Sam on the sidewalk. Her voice was low. "I know you have a problem with me."

Sam had to stop or he'd run right into her. "I don't know what you're talking about."

Destiny's lips twisted at the edges into a sly smile. "Yeah, you do."

Suddenly she put her small hands on his chest and pressed her body flat against him. "Just so you know, I've been thinking about you, too."

Then she abruptly took off toward the restaurant.

Sam forced himself to start walking again. One foot in front of the other. And he did his best to disappear inside himself, to become invisible to the world.

But at the corner, he couldn't help but look back over his shoulder.

And Destiny was there in the distance. Her face said one thing: *I'll be ready when you are. I'll be there.*

19

Clarence rode down the busy street on the stolen bike. Just six blocks away, on the left, he saw a prize: a farmers market. A smile cracked his too pale face.

We have a winner in aisle three.

Pushing the bicycle through the light crowd made up of women with strollers, elderly couples, and casual shoppers, Clarence came out on the other end of the street with a plastic bag, which held a woman's wallet. Over his arm was some-one's old green sweatshirt.

He also had two persimmons and the small lockbox from a careless and overwhelmed vendor.

Clarence pulled the sweatshirt over his head, and after taking the money, he dropped the lockbox into a trash can.

He smiled at a pretty teenage girl with red hair and told her, "Have a nice day." She blushed slightly and said, "You too."

As he got back on the bike he saw a flock of birds over-head. They were dancing in the sky.

He felt their joy. He felt their freedom. And if he had a gun, he'd have loved to wipe them right off the horizon. But he'd save the impulse for when it mattered.

*   *   *

Clarence had been out for twelve minutes when, inside the Merced Medical Center, Denny Piercey finally got tired of the long wait.

Denny knocked on the door. "Hurry it up in there!"

But there was no answer.

After several moments the guard turned the doorknob and, discovering that it was locked, tried the key.

But he had trouble. The key met some resistance. It no longer moved in the lock. Something was blocking the cylinder.

Denny was now alarmed. "Open the door. Right now!"

But from inside there was only the sound of running water.

Denny returned to the doctor's office and asked for another key. It took more than five minutes for the receptionist to find one.

The prison guard, now very agitated, radioed for help, requesting that the Merced city police set up a perimeter check around the building as a precaution for a "possible situation."

Four patrol cars responded, and eight minutes later, two officers, with Piercey at their side, knocked down the bathroom door.

By this point, Piercey wasn't surprised at the empty room and the open window.

But he still kicked the trash can in frustration. It hit the wall and ricocheted back.

The putrefied mouse rolled out onto the tile floor and landed at the prison guard's feet.

* * *

A mile away Clarence entered a drugstore and with money from the purloined wallet and lockbox purchased a kit of Clairol Knockout Blonde hair color.

He also got a bottle of vodka, navy-blue sweatpants, and a pair of sunglasses. At a gas station half a mile farther, Clarence spent twenty minutes in a locked bathroom dyeing his black hair into what turned out to be a coppery version of Knockout Blonde.

He drank two inches of vodka from the bottle, removed his government-issue work pants, and pulled on the navy sweats. He finished by slipping on his new sunglasses.

Clarence appeared to be nothing like the man who had gone into the medical center only an hour before.

And for the first time since his operation, his phantom foot gave him some peace.

Maybe, he thought, the pain was all in his head.

Layers of wailing sirens, like a shrill chorus singing in a round, could be heard in the distance.

Clarence knew that they were looking for him.

But his secret was to continue to hide in plain sight.

* * *

Clarence ditched his bike in the trees behind the gas station. He then bought a ticket to an action film at the City Place Stadium Cinema complex right on Main Street. With a tub of popcorn and a box of Junior Mints, he found a seat in the middle of the theater.

As the coming attractions played, Clarence shut his eyes and allowed himself to soak in his success.

He would now spend two hours watching spaceships destroy the great cities of the world with the help of robots that had turned against humanity and joined the alien invaders.

It was heaven on earth.

And just what he needed.

20

The boys were alone in the house in the middle of the day when the doorbell rang.

Riddle was in the living room, carefully looking at one of his learn-to-read books. Jared was upstairs avoiding him.

Felix the dog immediately started barking with the kind of urgency he only exhibited in the middle of the day, giving Jared the opportunity to shout at the top of his lungs: "Answer it, Riddle!" It made him feel like the boss if he could tell the alien space invader what to do. But Riddle was already up before Jared even got the last syllable out.

Riddle opened the door to find Beto Moreno standing on the porch. He went to school with Jared and could run faster and jump higher than kids two years older than him. This was just one of the reasons Beto was the most popular person in his class.

Jared had been working on winning Beto over as his best friend for years, but so far none of his efforts had succeeded.

Even giving Beto his gaming system on extended loan didn't change his attitude.

Riddle now found Beto holding a shopping bag. "I'm dropping this off. Jared wanted me to try it out."

Riddle took everything literally. "You tried out a bag?"

Beto smiled. "Yeah. But with an Xbox inside it."

Most people were afraid when Felix started barking and jumping, because Felix was a big dog. But Riddle noticed right away that Beto didn't seem at all intimidated. "I got bit once by a German shepherd, but it was my fault. I was running across the parking lot of a gas station, and I think he was trained to keep people from doing that."

Riddle looked down at the dog in a new way. "Maybe he's been trained to dig. He makes a lot of holes in the backyard."

Riddle decided that the kid looked friendly. And he knew Jared. So he said: "You can come into the house."

Beto stepped inside, laughing. "Yes, I can."

It was almost an hour later when Jared came downstairs to get a new battery for his robotic ball. Right away he heard talking.

Jared froze in his tracks to listen.

"You really can't read that?"

"No. I'm just learning the sounds. And that's too many letters."

"What kind of school did you go to?"

"I never went to school."

"No way."

"Yes. Way."

"So you were taught at home?"

"No."

"Were you raised by wolves or something?"

"There weren't any wolves. But I saw a bear up close once. And lots of other animals."

"You crack me up, Riddle."

"Thank you."

Jared instantly knew the voice. It was Beto's. What was *he* doing in the kitchen, talking to Riddle? This was crazy. But before Jared could get into the room to stop things, he heard:

"Riddle, you wanna come with me to the park? I've got batting practice in twenty minutes."

Jared couldn't believe it. All he'd ever wanted to do was hang out at the park with Beto. And now Beto was inviting *Riddle* to do that?

Life just wasn't fair.

* * *

The three boys ended up spending the rest of the day together. Riddle made chocolate tacos, which were waffles folded in half, stuffed with ice cream, and topped with nuts and cherries that were supposed to look like salsa.

He also gave his two cats a bath. Beto was fascinated watching Riddle wash the cats in the kitchen sink. Riddle made low cooing sounds that seemed to calm the felines, who submitted to the procedure with surprisingly little resistance.

131

Jared did his best to take every opportunity to point out how weird and strange Riddle was.

But it backfired.

It felt like the more Beto realized how *different* Riddle was, the more he was interested.

Finally, after hours of mounting an assault, Jared went silent when it was time to go over to the neighbors' house and feed the fish. Jared was certain that Beto would take off for home, but instead he crossed the yard with them and watched as Riddle removed the key from under the brick at the bottom of the Binghams' back stairs.

"How come you don't just take the key to your house and give it back to them when they get home?"

Jared couldn't help but snap, "They told us to do it this way."

Riddle knew Beto had a good point. People hid keys outside all the time. His father had been an expert in finding them. But that was a thought he didn't share.

*   *   *

Once inside, Riddle went straight to the fish tank.

Jared dropped to the couch. He was exhausted. Trying to cause trouble was a lot of work. Even when you weren't successful.

Beto walked around, going from room to room looking at the Binghams' stuff while Riddle shook the food flakes into the tank. The fish swam to the top of the water and greedily gobbled the floating meal.

Riddle thought back to all the times when he was hungry. His entire childhood until he met the Bells was one long wait for something to satisfy him.

Now, watching the fish, he couldn't stop himself. He stuck his fingers into the tin and took a big pinch and then put the food into his mouth.

It did not taste good.

It was salty. And sharp. It had a metallic edge, which surprised him.

Jared felt euphoric. This was exactly what he needed Beto to witness. But from across the room, Beto burst out laughing. "Did you just eat fish food?"

Riddle nodded as he carefully put the container back on the shelf.

Beto came closer. "Why?"

"I wanted to know how it tasted. It's not very good. It was like when you have a penny in your mouth."

Jared and Beto both watched as Riddle then picked up the mail off the floor where it had dropped from the slot. He organized it on the countertop in order of size.

He next checked the soil in the rubber tree plant and leaned close as he whispered to the broad, shiny leaves. "Tomorrow you will get a drink."

And then he headed for the door.

When they were outside, all Beto said was, "Riddle, if my family ever goes anywhere, I want you to watch over our house."

Riddle nodded. "Of course, Beto. I'd be happy to."

And that was the moment Jared knew the battle was over.

If watching the alien invader eat fish food didn't turn Beto, nothing would.

*　*　*

It was still hot outside long after the sun went down.

The heat had baked the town all day long, and upstairs at the Bells' house the rooms were all stuffy and too warm.

Emily didn't turn on the light in her room as she came in and took a seat on her bed. Sitting in the dark, she tried to figure out what was bothering her.

Why did it seem like a big deal to quit Ferdinand's?

Leo, the owner, didn't like her.

She hadn't gotten any better at juggling the barrage of requests that seemed to assault her at every shift.

Since she was only busing tables, not waiting them, the tips were just a fraction of what she had expected.

And there was the humiliation of getting locked inside the freezer, which still brought on daily teasing from the dishwashers and the cooks.

They didn't understand that the metal box still traumatized her.

And finally, Robb Ellis and now Destiny were both working there.

So she should have felt relief, even joy, to have an easy job with set hours where she could read a book when things got slow.

She would no longer have the stress of potentially scalding a person by spilling hot coffee, which had already happened once.

She should have felt grateful that her boyfriend had been looking out for her enough to go out in the world and find her a new job.

Sam had picked her up at the end of her shift, and he'd presented the whole plan as a done deal. Destiny's job was available, and now it was hers.

He had the telephone number of the woman from the gift shop for her. He said Emily would start the next day because the training was minimal.

But the truth behind it all was obvious: Sam didn't want Emily to work with Destiny. Or Robb Ellis. Maybe that's what was really bugging her.

Emily could hear Riddle in the hallway, explaining to Jared and his friend Beto that he wanted them to bake crescent rolls stuffed with peanut butter and jelly inside.

She couldn't see Jared's face, but she was certain that he wouldn't be interested in cooking anything. So she was surprised when she heard Jared say, "Okay, I can help you measure the stuff."

For a second their conversation took her mind away from Sam and the restaurant and her new job and Destiny.

But when she returned to that swirl of thoughts, she could suddenly see the dilemma in a different way.

Sam and Riddle had been so reliant on her family. They had basically been quiet, docile, and compliant.

But maybe that was changing now.

Maybe this was the time for the tables to turn.

It was possible that the strong ones weren't really that strong.

And perhaps the weak were tougher than it seemed.

21

The news outlets in California were reporting that a dangerous convict had fled earlier in the day from the Merced Medical Center.

But he had only one leg, and the circulating theory was that he was hiding somewhere on the grounds of the large health-care complex.

The Merced police department had sent its entire canine unit to a training session in San Francisco, so a request had been made to the division in Modesto. They were out in the field and would take two hours to get there.

Clarence's time in the theater had brought an unknown stroke of good luck that could never have been calculated. Or even wished for.

An Amtrak train had derailed going up the Central Corridor route, and there were injuries.

Local law enforcement suddenly switched their priority from looking for the criminal to aiding the sheriff's department in an emergency situation eighteen miles out of town.

That distraction, coupled with Clarence's ease at blending in, allowed him to shop for a new pair of jeans and a T-shirt, both nondescript but with a certain sense of style.

Looking good was always important.

And now that he had the copper-colored hair, he was going for a more Californian, upscale-urban presentation.

After he paid for the two items, he asked if the salesclerk could cut off the tags. He wanted to wear the outfit home to surprise the Wife.

Back in the dressing room, carefully putting on the new jeans after removing his artificial lower leg, he found the opportunity to slip a lightweight, cream-colored cashmere summer sweater under the tissue in the store bag.

Minutes later, outside on the street, with the expensive sweater slung casually over the new T-shirt, he strolled off to the best hotel in town. When he wanted to, he could walk without a limp. It was all a matter of focus.

In front of the hotel, Clarence made small talk with the doorman, explaining that he was waiting for his business partner.

When several cars arrived and the two overworked parking valets were both on the move, Clarence lifted a set of car keys from the never-locked lockbox that stood at the curb— the one that he'd been so casually standing next to.

He then went inside the hotel, exited through a door in the back, and entered the parking lot from the rear entrance.

He was pleased to see that his keys, marked with the number ninety-eight, matched a clean, silver, new-model Honda.

And even more rewarding was the fact that inside the vehicle were a large bottle of water, a bag of salt-and-vinegar potato chips, and a baseball cap. Clarence had claimed the car of a traveler, and if things continued to go his way, the owner wouldn't even try to collect the vehicle until the morning.

He put the keys in the ignition and drove out of the lot, giving a friendly wave to the valet, who barely even noticed him.

Clarence then traveled in the Honda up Route 99 to Stockton, picking up the northbound 5 Freeway. He pulled into Sacramento late that evening, parking on a side street with a nice view of the state capitol building.

He wanted to make a statement to the government.

Clarence Border was no longer a guest of the penal system.

22

It didn't take much for Destiny to get Robb Ellis to use his credit card for a weekly room at the Starlight Motel on West Sixth Street.

The place had a movie-star theme, but they were silver-screen heroes from long ago. Robb and Destiny didn't recognize any of them, and not just because the pictures pinned up behind the registration desk were really faded.

No movie actor or TV personality or even Internet sensation had ever set foot in the motel.

The original owners had put the names of their three favorite stars in the now cracked concrete walkway in the courtyard. Small pebbles spelled out the names Burt Reynolds, Donna Mills, and Richard Chamberlain. The little rocks were the size of jelly beans, and more than half of them were missing.

Destiny's room was in front of the pitted Donna Mills star. The accommodations featured a room with one tiny window and a bed that pretty much took up all the space, because you couldn't even open the door all the way without hitting the corner of the yellowy mattress.

Robb Ellis was creeped out by the whole place, but Destiny looked very happy and said that she'd pay him back once she got her first paycheck from the restaurant.

She also said that he could spend the night whenever he wanted.

He couldn't believe that part.

And so he went straight out the door to the front office and had the twitchy woman behind the desk charge him for two weeks, not one.

He'd think of something good to tell his parents when the credit-card bill came.

Like maybe that he helped a homeless person, because that was the truth.

And that got him thinking about whether this was something he could put on his college applications.

Maybe he would start a foundation to encourage teenagers to find ways to shelter homeless people and get them off the streets. If they were all as hot as Destiny, he imagined he could find lots of his friends to be part of the program.

But the first night didn't turn out the way he'd planned.

After they'd picked up Destiny's stuff from the dorm and moved it into the Starlight, she didn't want to strip down to her leopard underwear and roll around on the bed, like he'd imagined.

She said that she was too hungry.

So they went for cheeseburgers at Gary's Burger Shack.

They brought along a six-pack of beer from the market and somehow finished it all. Then Destiny said she was too tired to do so much as keep her eyes open and that she'd see him in the morning.

Before he knew it, Robb found himself outside, on the Donna Mills star. The light switched off in her room, and it was so dark that he couldn't see anything through the motel window.

As he walked to his SUV he decided that it was a good idea to take things slowly.

Robb looked up into the night sky, and right above him was a shooting star.

And he felt certain it was meant just for him.

23

Clarence met Lindy Braverman at a bar in downtown Sacramento called Smiling Faces.

He went in because of the name.

He figured only women with self-esteem issues would go to a pickup place with the audacity to call itself "Smiling Faces." And that was the kind of woman he needed to meet.

Lindy was a cat person, and that meant she had pet hair from her six beloved felines stuck in the creases and folds of most of her boldly patterned clothing. She was a walking hairball, and it was enough to give people sensitive to cat allergies attacks of prolonged sneezing.

But Lindy was unaware of this. She was unaware of many things.

So when the good-looking, gangly, copper-haired man leaned against the bar and almost purred, "Why don't you buy me a drink?" she did.

Her horoscope that morning had said it was a day to be bold and make new friends.

Several hours later, when the two were alone in Lindy's cramped apartment with just the cats, she didn't even notice that part of Clarence's left leg was man-made.

Lindy had had too much to drink, and she was too happy about the fact that Tom Baker, as the crazy-handsome man was named, was a Kings supporter. She had been wearing her Kings superfan underwear, and he had congratulated Lindy on her team choice.

Several hours later, when Clarence left Lindy Braverman's apartment at three thirty in the morning, he had an antique diamond ring that he'd taken from a small leather box in her underwear drawer, most of the cash that was in her wallet, and all the leftover prescription pain medication for her gum surgery, which was on the second shelf in the medicine cabinet.

And then, for the icing on the criminal cake, he opened a window in the kitchen to create a bigger distraction.

He gathered up Lindy's six beloved cats and herded them out onto the sidewalk. The two small ones ran right back to the closed door, terrorized to be outside in the dark of night.

The other four cats set off to explore the brave new world.

24

Emily woke up in the middle of the night and couldn't go back to sleep.

She couldn't remember ever having an enemy.

But wasn't that what Destiny now was?

Maybe *rival*, she thought, was a better word to describe the girl. They were competing for Sam's affection. Only, the crazy part was that Emily had already won.

He was hers.

Weren't she and Sam one?

Hadn't they already been tested?

Since the impossibly sexy Destiny had appeared, suddenly they were one plus the shadow of someone else. And it felt like they were three.

Was she imagining that?

No.

It was real.

When she and Sam were alone together after work, she

felt as if the magnetlike pull of emotion that brought them together had been blocked.

Or rearranged.

Some other element had entered the equation. And just because they weren't talking about it didn't mean it wasn't happening.

He was vulnerable. Emily knew that. He didn't have enough experience living a stable life. He was strong, but at the same time she could feel his weakness. It was real. It might lead him astray. It might ruin his life.

There was morning light in the sky when Emily finally fell back asleep. But the distant pink on the horizon was Destiny's favorite color.

At least that's what she had told Emily at the restaurant when she'd applied a smear of gloss over her large, pouty lips.

Before, Emily might have seen the sky as beautiful, but as she dozed back to sleep, her last thought was that the future light looked grim.

25

Law enforcement should have immediately informed the Bell family that Clarence Border was no longer incarcerated.

But he was in prison in California, and the Bells lived in Oregon.

And while Clarence had abducted his children and shot a firearm at both of them, he had not been classified as the highest level of violent offender.

His case had not yet gone to court, and because he was going to roll over on the charges and had a major disability with his amputated leg, he had been given a break in prison placement.

So while the story hit the press that an inmate had escaped while on a medical examination at the Merced Medical Center, and a description of Clarence with a photo made the news around the state, no large-scale manhunt captivated the public in Oregon.

Major news sources were consumed with the fact that the

current Miss America had been found naked in a donut-shop bathroom with the governor of Oregon.

The security tape of the incident had been posted online, and it was downloaded so many times that servers were crashing.

The nation's rival donut chain had immediately come out with a specialty pastry that mocked the incident. The appropriateness of that new food item was also being discussed in the mainstream press—adding fuel to the salacious fire.

And that kept the heat off Clarence.

*　*　*

The pawnshop trade was simple.

It was all about waiting and watching.

Clarence saw the guy go into the store with the box, which he was certain held a weapon. And he waited to see him come out with the same box still in hand.

He could see a person's intention by the slump of the shoulders. He knew what defeat looked like in a man's posture. A deal gone south.

Clarence got out of the car that he'd stolen in Sacramento and headed across the parking lot. It looked like a case of great timing that the two men should run into each other.

Clarence spoke in a soft voice. He had such clean hands, and he wore a cashmere sweater. He kept his fingers from strumming too intently on his thighs.

He was going into the shop to buy a firearm, he said to the man, and he wondered what it was like in there.

The weapon was not for himself, he added. He had no idea how to even use one. It was for his mother, who was feeling afraid in her home. She would never use it. She would never register it. It would be a prop. She wouldn't even leave the house, since her fall on the back stairs.

She'd given him money for the gun. He had her cash right here, in fact. He fanned out hundreds in his left hand.

The dejected man was happy to help.

It happened quickly, and both sides felt good about what they'd done. Wasn't that the definition of a square deal?

When both sides are smiling?

26

Destiny had let Robb Ellis sleep over on her second night at the Starlight Motel. He was, after all, paying for the place.

But he bored her, and not just because he talked a lot about nothing, but because he was so easy to figure out.

Destiny could imagine getting the guy to build an altar to her image. He already said that he wanted to take her to Hawaii, which was a place she'd never been but of course always wanted to visit.

But that promise was for when he graduated from high school, which was something like a year off.

If it were maybe three weeks away, she would have laughed more at his jokes.

· Now, as she sat on the edge of the bed waiting for her newly applied orange toenail polish to dry, Destiny's face scrunched up. She had a way of not wanting anything she had (which wasn't much) and desiring everything she didn't have (which was plenty).

Robb Ellis was only several feet away, but he could have been in another state.

"I told my parents I slept over at Rory's."

She could hear his voice, but the words didn't penetrate any more than the ceiling fan did.

"I'm going to say that I'll be at Nick's tonight."

Destiny nodded. He was like a radio that was tuned to the Dull Station.

Destiny got to her feet and carefully slipped her not-yet-dry toes into a pair of rubber sandals. Robb Ellis looked over. "You can't wear sandals to work."

Destiny then grabbed her purse out of a pile of handbags. Today's choice was a pink, fluffy thing that looked like a stuffed animal.

"I'm going," she said.

Robb was still staring at her feet. "I think it's because of the health code or something. The sandals."

Destiny looked at Robb Ellis now for the first time since she'd pushed him away and taken three steps into the mildewed shower, where she'd happily stayed until the last drop of hot water was gone.

"What are you saying?"

Robb cleared his throat. "You can't wear the sandals to the restaurant."

But Destiny's hand was on the doorknob, and she pulled to open the entrance.

Hard light flooded the room, making it look suddenly tiny and tattered and cheap, which Destiny now realized it was.

"I'm not going to work," she said. "You don't have a day shift. Cover for me."

And then Robb watched as she disappeared straight out the door.

* * *

Clarence headed north.

He bought a sleeping bag, a foam pad, and a small tent at the Walmart in Redding. At a gas station later in the day, he lifted a map and located a campground, where he staked out a spot with as much privacy as he could find.

He drank vodka, smoked cigarettes, ate a plastic bucket of teriyaki-style beef jerky, and passed out with his shoes and his artificial leg still on. His newly acquired handgun was under his rolled-up cashmere sweater.

He slept for almost twenty-four straight hours.

Since it was summer, families invaded the outdoors with mountains of crap and armies of undisciplined kids on the weekends.

Clarence emerged from his tent in the afternoon in a rumpled daze to find a six-year-old kid peeing on one of his tent stakes.

He wanted to teach the soft brat a lesson, but then the voices inside stopped him.

It's not worth it.

If he were going to hit a kid—and he was—it would be his own damn kid. And it would be a teaching moment Sam and Riddle could never forget.

* * *

Clarence spent two days at the state park, soaking in the beautiful fact that there was now darkness in his life.

And silence.

At least at night, when the yapping kids and their heavily drinking parents finally passed out.

He shut his eyes and didn't feel the hot burn of the over-head fluorescent tubing that was 24-7 prison lighting.

The voices in his head weren't interrupted by the rants of his fellow inmates. Bandit couldn't be heard trading a tortilla for a piece of tinfoil.

It was a miracle.

He was one step ahead of the haters.

Maybe two.

He would continue north.

Moving to his goal.

It was a piece of good luck that the Bell family lived in Oregon, not Arizona. Everyone knew that it was better to be a criminal in colder climates. In cool places, you can hide a damaged mind and an evil soul and an artificial leg.

But north really meant the one thing, above all, that his life was now about.

Sam and Riddle.

And the Bell family.

Clarence felt his blood pressure literally rise.

It was payback time, people.

27

He was back in school.

Sam sat in English Composition Skills and waited for class to begin.

The windows were open in the lecture hall, which was only one-third full, and a warm summer breeze, which smelled like fried onions, drifted into the room. They were dangerously close to the student union, and half the time the classroom was like a food truck.

Sam was bracing himself for the fact that he was going to have to write the first paper of his life in only a week. The idea terrorized him.

But what didn't terrorize him right now?

He was trying as hard as possible to keep on track.

Scattered in the rows directly in front of him was a collection of students, who, for varying reasons, were all forced to take what in the catalog was known as English 101, or Bonehead English, according to the guy who sat behind him.

During summer session a handful of huge guys who were on the football team took the class so that they could have a lighter load during the season. There was a big group of English-as-a-second-language students. There were a few kids with medical problems, who were now trying to catch up on credits. And then there was Sam.

Just as everyone was settling in, he looked over to see someone talking to the professor out in the hallway.

The Someone turned, revealing the kind of body that was used to sell underwear and perfume. It was all curves.

That Someone did not belong in the lecture hall.

But she was coming in.

Someone took a seat in the back of the room. Sam could feel her eyes on him. But he would not—he could not—acknowledge that she was there.

For the rest of the ninety-minute class, Sam stared straight ahead, more absorbed than he'd ever been in the technique of diagramming sentences. He watched as the professor circled nouns and verbs and adverbs and adjectives.

He wrote down almost everything the teacher said, concentrating on the front of the classroom, the light fixtures above the whiteboard, and the crimped quality of Professor Hunt's handwriting, which was projected up onto a large screen.

And then finally, after forever, the class was over, and Sam gathered up his things and shoved them all into his backpack, never looking even once to see if Someone was still behind him.

Only one entrance of Addison Hall was open in the summer, so he had to go out the front door.

But of course she was right on his heels. She immediately hollered out, "Hey, you're a real student. I saw how you were writing stuff down. I couldn't understand half of what the lady was saying. I had no idea you were Mr. Scholar."

Several of the thick-necked football guys laughed, and one of the ESL students murmured, "Mr. Scholar."

But Sam didn't acknowledge her.

Destiny hopped after him. "Don't you want to hear how I knew you were in class?"

Sam shook his head. "Nope." And he kept walking. But she stayed right with him, at his elbow now.

They looked, to the outside world, like a couple. Only, because he was rigid and stared straight ahead, they appeared to be a pair who had just had a fight.

She continued. "You hungry?"

He was starving, but he answered, "No."

She smiled. "You are just the worst liar."

Sam stopped. His feet seemed to freeze to the walkway, and he now faced her. "What do you want from me?"

Destiny grinned. She had him now. He had stopped. He was angry, but he was talking to her. "I want to get to know you better."

"Why?"

"I just do. I feel like we might have stuff in common. My dad's in jail. So is yours. That's a start."

"How did you know that?"

"Robb. He tried to make himself into some kind of crime fighter. He told the whole story of how you met Emily and then just disappeared because your dad was mental. My dad's in jail for stealing cars. But he's a nice guy. When he was around, that is."

"And your mom?" Sam heard himself asking.

Destiny broke his gaze. "Pushing up daisies. What about yours?"

"Same," Sam mumbled.

Destiny grinned at him. She had his full attention. And he no longer was some kind of rage machine.

She whispered, but loud enough for him to hear: "Girls choose. You know that, right?"

He tried to keep his eyes on her face. He didn't want to look at her clinging, low-cut top that had nothing but skin underneath. Or stare at her short-shorts.

He shifted his weight as he answered. "Choose what?"

"Girls choose guys. Boys think they're in charge, but they're not. We decide."

Sam sounded defeated. "I don't think I'm in charge of anything."

Destiny smiled. "Clearly."

* * *

Sam was lying in the dark staring up at the ceiling and wondering how it happened that he'd driven Destiny back to the Starlight Motel.

Why did they stop first at Tommy's Market, and why did she come out with not just shampoo, like she'd said she had to buy, but with a six-pack of beer?

Why did he sit in the car and allow her to drink a bottle?

And why, when he told her that he was in love with Emily, and that he belonged to a family now and everything that he'd ever dreamed of had come true, did she laugh at him?

Why?

And when, in the late light of the afternoon (with the red spill from the neon sign that said *Starlight Motel* burning in through the side window), why did he just sit there when she got out of her seat and straddled his lap and kissed him, full on the lips, like some kind of wild, wounded animal?

Why had he not stopped her before that happened?

Even when he finally got her off him and out of the car, why could he still taste her beer breath?

Why could he still smell that oil she put behind her ears that was musky and pungent like fresh-cut hay put in an old barn?

Why was it that sometimes things that were rotten smelled sweet?

28

Sam didn't ask himself the most important question, which was: why did Emily happen to drive by and see it all happen?

He didn't ask, because he didn't know she had. His eyes had momentarily shut, and he had a woman's body pressing into him. Destiny wasn't there for long before he pushed her away.

But Emily had driven by just as Destiny wedged her small but shockingly full figure between the steering wheel and Sam.

Emily drove by just when his lips were locked to hers.

She was in her father's car, because she'd heard from Nora, who had heard from her boyfriend, Rory, that Destiny was living at the Starlight Motel with Robb Ellis. Or at least that he'd spent a few nights there and lied to his parents.

Emily wanted to see the place.

Sam had class, and she was waiting for him to call her when he was done. But she hadn't heard from him, so she decided to surprise Jared and Riddle and Beto and go get pistachio gelato, which was a special flavor at the little Italian ice-cream place downtown.

Did Emily know that going to the gelato shop meant that she could drive by the Starlight? Of course.

She thought she might spot Destiny. And maybe Robb Ellis.

But she didn't expect to see her car, the one Sam drove, parked right in front of the dumpy little motor court.

And she didn't think that she'd see her boyfriend, the love of her life, her reason for living, the most beautiful person in the world on the inside and the outside that she'd ever met, sitting in the driver's seat with a girl on his lap.

No.

She didn't expect that.

* * *

It was too good to be true.

That's an expression.

It was too good to be true.

One more time.

Too.

Good.

To.

Be.

True.

Which is another way of saying not true.

Which is another way of saying false.

Which is another way of saying liar.

Okay. Liar. Liar. Liar.
O. O. O.
Oh. Oh. Oh.

*　*　*

Emily's brain went on pause. It stopped thinking about Sam and Destiny and thought only of how to make it home without crashing the car.

Red means stop.

And green means go.

You do what you are supposed to do.

You believe in the system, because it is set up and it works and you are supposed to believe in things.

You are supposed to stay in the lanes when you drive, and you are supposed to drive a certain speed in certain areas and that's not too fast and not too slow.

And you can count on the other people in their cars to do that, too.

Because there are rules, and one of the rules is that you follow the rules.

You follow the rules, because if you don't follow the rules, then there are consequences.

*　*　*

Emily put her foot on the brake and pulled her father's Subaru to the curb. If her dad had driven to work instead of taking his bike, then she wouldn't have been able to go for ice cream. And then she wouldn't have driven by the motel. And she wouldn't have seen what she saw.

Was this all her father's fault?

Emily reached over and looked at the brown paper bag with the pistachio gelato hand-packed in a white cardboard container. A single, thick rivulet of icy, sick-green goo oozed out of the top and ran down the side.

She lifted the bag and now saw that the bottom of the brown sack was wet. So part of the gelato didn't want to be in the container.

It wanted to get out.

Or maybe it wasn't packed right, and that part never was in the container.

She looked more carefully, and everything in the entire universe was now focused on the pistachio gelato and the brown sack.

And then it all made sense.

She lifted out the container, and she could see that there was a split in the seam.

It had looked like a container that worked. But it was damaged. No one had seen that.

But now, yes. Now it was obvious.

Still holding the container, she watched a drop of liquid hit the cardboard top.

One and then two.

The tears streaked down her cheeks and were silent as they dropped from her chin.

Calmly, carefully, precisely, Emily opened the car door and dropped the gelato and the brown bag onto the street.

Out of the car, out of her life.

She had never littered like this before. She knew it wasn't right.

But she didn't care.

Then she shut the car door and put her foot on the gas and drove straight home.

29

Emily didn't see the silver car parked just down the street when she pulled into the driveway.

Her eyes were functioning, but the images in front of her had no meaning. She had lost the ability to see detail, which was her gift. Now the world was just shapes.

But there was a car parked under a tree. And there was a man in the front seat.

He was very still, with his head sucked straight back into the headrest.

The man watched as Emily pulled the Subaru into the brick driveway and then entered the house through the kitchen door.

Her gaze was downcast.

He couldn't see much more without getting out of his car, and he wasn't going to do that.

No. He was going to wait and watch and understand what was happening inside the Bell house.

And then he'd make his move.

* * *.

The three boys had spent almost the whole day digging in the Bells' backyard.

The fish tank in the Binghams' house had inspired an idea.

They were going to work together to dig a pond behind the garage.

They would fill it with water and then see if they could get fish to live there and maybe make money from neighbor kids who wanted to take fishing lessons.

But they weren't going to have tropical fish or salt water or heat lamps. Just regular water from the green garden hose and probably goldfish. Jared wanted eels, but Beto couldn't believe that would work.

So they made a deal to figure out the fish later. Today had been about the three of them trying to dig a pond, and that was harder than it looked. It was summer, and the ground was pretty dry even though they did have a sprinkler back there.

They'd been at it for hours when they finally quit and went into the house. They were covered in dirt and exhausted, but getting along. Beto was the glue holding them all together.

And then Emily had said that she was going to go buy them a treat. Hadn't she asked what their favorite flavor of gelato was?

But she didn't bring them anything.

She came back but didn't even look at them or talk

about the fish-pond progress. Instead she went right up to her room.

* * *

It wasn't long before Riddle announced that it was time to do their chores at the neighbors' house.

Jared took the key from under the loose bricks. But he was tired and careless, and it slipped through his fingers. Riddle bent down and picked it up.

For some reason, the lock was stiff, and they had trouble opening the door. They struggled, but finally Beto got the deadbolt to move. He pulled the doorknob hard against his body, and it worked.

They were all hungry and wanted to get the job done fast, and so Beto fed the fish and Jared took care of the mail. Riddle went to check on the plants.

He found that the rubber tree plant at the front window was dry. Riddle was surprised, because he'd watered it only two days before.

A wave of bad feeling washed over him.

Riddle decided that the plant was too close to the glass. The light came in low and strong at the end of the day. And so he bent down and pulled on the rim of the pot.

And when he did, his peripheral vision detected movement. In the bushes. Along the side of the house.

Was something there? An animal?

Was someone watching?

Riddle pushed his new glasses farther up the bridge of his nose and looked out at the street. It was quiet. Only a single new silver car was parked on the whole block. No one was inside the vehicle. There was nothing but late-afternoon sunlight and summer heat out there.

Before he could investigate further, he heard Jared holler from the kitchen that they were leaving.

But minutes later, when they were all back outside, Riddle noticed that the light was still on in the kitchen. The Binghams were pretty strict. They had timers for the fixtures and wanted their house to always look the same at night.

So Jared again got the key from underneath the loose brick. The house seemed more vacant the second time they went in.

Riddle walked over to the saltwater tank, and the fish that he liked the most, the transparent one that always hid behind the coral, wiggled out. It came right up to the glass.

Riddle bent down close to get a better look, and the fish darted away. It was there, and then suddenly gone.

Moments later Riddle was back with the two boys, heading across the lawn to the Bells' home.

He wished that fish could talk.

He felt certain that the little see-through guy was trying to tell me something.

*   *   *

At first Clarence didn't even recognize Riddle.

The boy was wearing glasses.

What was that about? The kid could see fine. More than fine.

It wasn't just the crazy orange eyewear that made him look so different. His wheat-colored hair had grown out. That could be expected. But he had a real cut—a style—which was strange.

You couldn't get that kid to do anything, so how did that happen?

But it wasn't the glasses or the haircut or the striped T-shirt or the fancy running shoes that made the most impact. It was the way he moved. That had changed. His head was raised now when he walked. He wasn't just staring down at the ground.

Riddle was part of something. And that made no sense. He was with two boys. Not Sam. And they all knew one another well. He could see that.

Clarence watched the trio cross the brick driveway. They were laughing. All of them.

But that wasn't right, because Riddle didn't laugh. He didn't talk and he didn't laugh and he didn't wear glasses. And now he was doing all of those things.

Then it struck him.

Riddle looked . . . normal.

That was the only way to describe it.

For an instant—just a flash of a moment—Clarence wanted to shout to the world, "That's my son."

But the pride, or the realization that his flesh and blood was doing okay, vanished as quickly as it had surfaced.

And it was replaced by anger.

And then silent rage.

*   *   *

Clarence watched the boys from the shadows.

He had moved silently, with only the barest perception of a limp, to the tall shrubs on the side of the house. And it was there, hidden by the thick leaves of the foliage, that he'd listened.

He'd heard enough to figure out that they were in charge of feeding something.

And only seconds after they'd disappeared through the Bells' back door, Clarence had the key out from under the brick and he was inside the neighboring house.

Score.

This required a change in the plan. Why not spend the night in a decent bed? Why not cook one of the steaks that was in the freezer and drink the expensive brandy from the fully stocked bar in the living room?

Upstairs he rifled through the medicine cabinets and found Percodan prescribed for a knee surgery. He popped two into his mouth and felt a swirl of happiness.

And then, moving in the long shadows of the hallway, he went to the bedroom window and looked out.

More good luck.

He could see right into the house next door.

The Girl.

She was slumped forward, sitting on her bed. And her head was heavy in her hands.

Happy people don't do that.

He watched and was excited to see something else. She was crying.

And that made him laugh. Loud and hard.

30

Sam had never felt this ashamed or guilty.

He drove to his apartment, and he took a long shower to wash off what felt like dirt, but nothing was there. He scrubbed his legs and held his head under the hot water until his skin was fiery red.

He wanted to call Emily. To be with her. He needed to hold her and tell her everything that had happened.

But he was gripped with fear.

What if she didn't want to see him anymore? What if she felt so betrayed that she needed him out of her life? What if he had now lost it all?

It was still light out, but he climbed into bed and shut his eyes just to rest. He needed a few minutes for the shouting in his head to stop. A nap.

A way to escape from himself.

* * *

When Sam opened his eyes, he knew right away that it was late.

He sat up in bed and immediately felt worse, not better. He'd done something wrong. Very wrong.

He reached down and picked up his phone, expecting to see a list of calls from Emily. And then text messages. She had to be looking for him.

But she wasn't.

And that was as strange as anything else that had happened in the day.

Sam slipped out from under the sheet and put on his jeans and a T-shirt.

He stepped into a pair of flip-flops that Emily had given him and he walked out the front door.

* * *

The clock showed that it was 2:46 AM.

And Riddle was awake.

He took his glasses from the table next to the bed and quietly got up to go to the bathroom. He didn't want to disturb Jared. Or Felix. But both of them were still snoring when Riddle stepped into the hall.

Right away something felt wrong.

It was brighter than usual.

Riddle looked up and saw that the small, round window at the end of the hallway glowed. And that only happened when the lights were on at the Binghams' house next door.

But the Binghams weren't going to be back from vacation until next Thursday.

Could they have come home early?

He knew for a fact that the light hadn't been on when he went to sleep. So either the Binghams were home before they said they were going to be...

Or someone was in their house.

*   *   *

Since it was summer, the air, even late, was still warm. But tonight it felt heavy. Moisture from a storm on another continent had blown across the Pacific Ocean. It had crossed the Cascade Mountains and then swept into the Willamette Valley, raising the humidity and making the whole town feel sticky.

Windows were open, and fans were on. As Sam walked down the sidewalk, he could hear the hum of seldom-used air conditioners.

Every step forward was a challenge. He wanted to do the right thing and tell Emily what had happened with Destiny. But he also wanted to simply disappear.

If he knew that Riddle would be okay, and that Emily and the Bells wouldn't go through pain trying to find him, that was what he'd do.

He would leave town and never come back. He wasn't good enough to be loved by Emily Bell. And he never would be.

But he wasn't even man enough to go.

So he walked down the empty streets toward her house, wrestling with how to explain himself. He decided that he would tell her exactly what had happened. And then he would ask for forgiveness.

As he worked his way through his plan, he was flooded with new anxiety.

Why hadn't she called him? Was something already wrong? They saw each other every day. They spoke nearly every hour and sent text messages when they were apart.

He had been so concerned about himself that he hadn't stopped to think about her side of things.

He started moving faster now. It was too late to call the house. Everyone would be asleep. But he had a key. He'd let himself in. He'd make sure that his family was all right.

And then he stopped.

He was right in front of the Bells' house, and there was no mistaking what he saw.

The beam of a flashlight moved in the backyard.

Someone was there.

An intruder.

Suddenly all doubt disappeared. He would do anything to protect the people in this house.

There was a shovel leaning against the garage. He could see it. Someone had been digging in the yard, and there were tools left out.

A shovel was a powerful thing. He's seen his father cut

the head clean off a rattlesnake by coming down hard right on the unsuspecting reptile.

Sam moved silently in the shadows to get his weapon. In seconds he had the shovel in hand. He raised it high in the air, ready to use the large metal scoop as a blade.

And then the beam of light poked through the purple-black right in front of him.

And he heard:

"Sam...?"

His tense body doubled down in adrenaline. He knew that voice.

The light beam jerked and shifted up to Sam's face, and Riddle could be heard: "You scared me!"

Sam was blinded by the flashlight, but he realized that he was now looking right at his little brother. Sam's voice was hard. "What are you doing out here?"

Riddle moved the light away to the grass. He adjusted his glasses. "What are *you* doing out here?"

Sam lowered the shovel, his muscles twitching as he realized how close he had come to attacking his own brother. "Riddle, you're not supposed to be outside with a flashlight at three in the morning!"

They both suddenly lowered their voices to whispers. "I saw a light on at the Binghams' house."

Sam's problems with Destiny had momentarily been wiped clean. "So what?"

Riddle took a step closer to his brother. "They aren't home. There shouldn't be a light on in there."

Sam looked up at the neighboring house. Something was, in fact, illuminating rooms upstairs.

"They're on vacation. Me and Jared are looking after the place. We didn't leave a light on. We don't ever even go upstairs. I think someone's in the house."

Sam glanced from his little brother back to the Binghams' second floor. "No one's up there."

Riddle aimed his flashlight behind the house. "I wanna go look. We hide the key back there."

Sam was insistent. "No. You're going inside to bed."

The harsh tone of Sam's voice reminded them both suddenly of their father. That sent a chill down their spines. The old Riddle would have turned and gone right back into the house. The new Riddle stood his ground.

"How come you weren't here for dinner? Emily didn't feel good. She didn't even come downstairs."

Sam cleared his throat as panic came back full force. His answer lacked conviction. "I was tired from school. I fell asleep. I just woke up."

Riddle looked up into his brother's eyes. He saw that something was wrong. "Sam...is everything okay?"

Sam put out his arm and motioned toward the house. "Go on. Get back to bed."

Riddle stared up at him. "Are you coming in?"

Sam leaned the shovel against the house.

"No. I'm going back to the apartment now. I'll be over first thing in the morning. I'll see you then."

Riddle didn't respond. But the look on his face made it clear to Sam that he was unhappy.

Riddle crossed the grass and disappeared through the back door into the Bell house. He walked to the window, but his brother was gone.

*   *   *

Sam stood on the sidewalk and stared up at the Binghams' house.

There was light coming from a window of the second floor, and for a moment it seemed as if something moved in the shadows.

Did he imagine that?

Sam's mind was a jumble now as he headed to the Binghams' walkway and proceeded up the two stairs to the porch and the large, dark windows.

He put his face right against the glass. There was a bluish glow coming from the aquarium in the den, but otherwise nothing could be seen but the vague shapes of furniture.

Sam moved to the front door, and there he thought he smelled broiled steak. He stepped back and the smell disappeared.

But if he stood right next to the door, by the little sliding peephole, the smell returned.

Had someone been cooking inside? No burglar would broil a steak.

The Binghams had to have returned early. That was the only explanation.

Down the street a car suddenly turned the corner and, as it drove past, the headlights brightened the area and Sam could see a silver sedan parked at the curb one house down.

That car had California license plates.

California.

When Clarence had hauled them around like bruised fruit, they'd spent a lot of time in that state.

The thought of his father pulled Sam away from the Binghams.

It brought him back to who he really was. The damaged son of a crazy person. He didn't belong here.

Sam stepped off the porch onto the walkway and then headed down the sidewalk.

But when he was at the end of the block, ready to cross the street, something made him turn and look over his shoulder.

That was when he knew for certain that his messed-up mind was shattered.

Because there was now a figure on the Binghams' front porch.

A body stood in silhouette.

And even from almost a block away, that thin, tall man was recognizable as his father.

* * *

Clarence held a gun.

He had missed an opportunity.

And by just seconds.

He could feel his heart racing, and it wasn't just from the cocktail of the Binghams' alcohol and prescription drugs.

His adrenaline had surged when he'd heard his sons' voices.

Both of them. Right outside.

But it took him too long to realize that the sounds weren't in his head.

The two traitors were standing in his driveway.

Yes, he thought of it as *his* property already.

He could have emerged from the house and taken them both down before they knew what hit them. His aim was good enough.

But he'd pulled off his fake leg earlier in the night, and now he hopped around the room, scrambling for his gun, his anger building as his pulse quickened.

By the time he got downstairs and outside, they were gone.

He'd seen the older boy take off down the street. It was after three in the morning, and no one awake at that hour could be doing anything to be proud of.

The kid had his head down and was walking like he was filled with shame. As he should be.

Clarence turned back to the house. The warm bed was waiting upstairs. The Bells would be there in the morning. And so would he.

31

Destiny stared at Robb Ellis's bare back.

He had a collection of moles that were scattered like flecks of dark brown paint on his olive skin.

She didn't like moles. But what she really didn't like was body hair. And Robb Ellis had a patch of brown strands—fur, really, was what it looked like—at the base of his spine.

Because of the heat of summer, the nubby polyester blanket and the gray-white sheet barely touched his body.

Destiny found herself staring at the triangle-shaped hair and wondering if he'd had a tail removed. Because it looked like the perfect spot for one to have been placed.

Destiny shut her eyes and tried to forget about the kid's possible additional appendage. There was nothing really wrong with Robb Ellis, but now that he had morphed into a primate, she needed to get away from him.

Especially since he was now snoring. Or moaning in his sleep. Or something fairly creepy.

And so she slowly, carefully, slid her toned legs out of bed. The room was so small that she could pull a dress over her head and slide into her orange slipper-shoes without taking a single step.

Her hand went for the doorknob, when she had another thought.

Robb's SUV was out front. She could take the car and drive to get coffee and maybe Sausage McMuffins or some kind of sugary donut. He wouldn't mind. He was asleep.

If she got back quickly, he wouldn't even know—right?

* * *

Destiny hopped into the Ellismobile, as Robb called his gas-guzzling SUV, and moved the seat all the way forward. But she still had trouble reaching the gas pedal. So she grabbed the Kleenex box, which Robb kept under the seat, because real guys don't blow their noses or something.

She did a fine job of smashing the cardboard down onto the tissues as she perched on top of the rectangle and pulled out into traffic.

It was a beautiful summer morning. Warm sun. Slight breeze.

All good.

Destiny pushed a finger on Robb's iPod, which was wired into his surround-sound-fancy stereo system, and music blared from all the speakers. Awesome.

Destiny considered one of her greatest strengths to be her

ability to come up with a new plan without deliberation or indecision of any kind.

Now, as she drove down Oak Street, she switched her destination and her motivation.

Forget the coffee and the sausage sandwich. Never mind the gooey Cinnabon.

Destiny wanted to start the day by seeing where her former rival lived. Because that's how she now saw pretty Emily Bell.

The night before, when Robb Ellis had shown up at the motel beer-soaked and clingy, Destiny got him to tell her again about Sam and Emily. But this time she wanted all the details. Not just the part where Robb was a hero.

So she'd heard the whole story of a kid who had a criminal father and no mother. She listened intently to how they had met when Emily sang at church and how her family had taken in the boys. And while her heart went out to Sam, his story made her want to know Emily.

The girl whose family had come to the rescue of the two boys was now impossibly intriguing.

Sam was just another bad-luck kid. Like her.

But Emily was something a whole lot more interesting. She was some kind of savior.

Destiny's new infatuation was sealed when Robb admitted that he'd been hung up on Emily himself at one point, but of course that had passed.

And when Destiny pressed, he'd told her exactly where Emily Bell lived. He'd rattled off the address on Agate Street and even described the house with the large front porch and the herringbone-brick driveway.

It was 242 Agate. She remembered because twenty-four was her favorite number.

Now Destiny punched in the address on the navigation system, stepped on the gas, and headed across town with the warm sun on her bare left arm and a boy band singing a song about the hand of fate.

*   *   *

Once Destiny was on the right street, she didn't even need the GPS to tell her where to go. The Bell house was exactly what she'd pictured when she'd dreamed about a real home.

It was good-size, with a sense of history. It had traditional style and elegant proportion. There were blooming flowerbeds in the front, and the large trees on either side of the property provided a natural frame when the house was viewed from the curb.

But it wasn't flashy architecture or a dramatic piece of land that made it all so appealing. It was the sense that the whole place was so cared for.

Closer inspection brought Destiny's eye to the long driveway, which led to a carriage-house-style garage in the back, where she could see a basketball hoop and a raised vegetable garden in a series of redwood boxes.

Destiny was right in the middle of absorbing the details of the six different wire funnels covered with tomato plants when she saw a man appear from the back of the house next door.

She was far away but could see that he was tall and thin. He walked stiff-legged, like his hips didn't move right. Or something wasn't moving right, because he limped.

Destiny took one look at him, and with her trained eye she could tell even from a distance that he was trouble.

And so she pulled the Kleenex box out from under her and slid down. She could now still see, but to anyone outside the car, it would be difficult to discern that a person was in the front seat.

Destiny watched as the tall figure slid through the bushes that separated his house from where Emily lived.

The man had something in his right hand, but it was hidden.

Destiny watched as he emerged from the bushes and moved across the brick driveway to the shrubs next to the Bells' house.

Even though he was mostly concealed, she could tell that he was peering in through the side window.

Destiny was riveted. She was spying on someone spying.

How cool was that?

But why was he snooping around Emily's house? He was the neighbor.

Well, what if he wasn't the neighbor? Maybe he was a burglar, and maybe she was witnessing a crime. And maybe, if she paid attention, she'd be involved in catching the guy.

And what if that led to some kind of reward?

Destiny moved closer to the car window, and her eyes never left the house.

* * *

Emily stayed in her room until she heard both of her parents' cars leave for work.

The boys were still asleep, and she knew they'd stay that way for hours.

She felt more tired than when she'd climbed into bed eight hours before, but she forced herself to get up.

The gnawing feeling from what she'd seen in the car in front of the Starlight Motel chewed away at the lining of her stomach. At the same time, it clouded her mind.

She was anxious and yet in a daze. She couldn't remember ever feeling that emotional combination.

Emily picked up her cell phone, which she'd forgotten to recharge, and stared at the icon that showed a red battery, not a green one, and displayed the words *Low Battery*.

Then the whole thing shut down.

Black screen.

Done.

It was almost a relief to be cut off from the world.

Once dressed, she went downstairs to the kitchen. Emily had no appetite but forced herself to drink a glass of orange juice.

She was struck by the fact that she usually found it so sweet, but now it was bitter.

There was a note on the counter that said:

Emily—Tell Sam we'll be doing BBQ tonight
and he should be here at 6.

She crumpled the piece of paper into a ball and threw it
in the trash.

Emily thought about calling Nora and asking if she could
come over, but she didn't feel like spilling her heart out, even
to her best friend.

She stared out the window at the rosebushes and finally
realized that she hadn't blinked in so long that her eyes felt
sticky-dry.

The clock on the wall said that even if she left right now,
she'd be late for work at the gift shop. She couldn't stand the
place. Destiny was right about that.

And so, with her mind in a fog, Emily grabbed her dead
cell phone and her charger, tossed them in her purse, and
walked out the back door.

And straight into Clarence Border.

*　　*　　*

The thin man had disappeared from Destiny's view.

What was he doing?

And then she saw him again.

He appeared, but now Emily was at his side. He had his
hand on her arm.

Tight.

But something was now very, very wrong. Destiny was
certain of it.

Emily's face said terror.

The man was talking as they walked, not slow but not fast.

Destiny watched as they moved down the driveway and onto the sidewalk and then made their way to a parked silver car. The man opened the passenger door, and Emily got inside the vehicle.

And it was then, for just a flash of a second, that Destiny could see what was in the man's right hand.

It was a gun.

It was pressed into Emily's side.

Destiny waited until the silver car pulled away from the curb, and then she sat up in the driver's seat, turned over the ignition, and swung around in a sweeping U-turn.

She was going after them.

32

The book Sam had read called *Starting Over: Life After Years of Abuse* said that guilt causes confusion.

And confusion leads to irrationality.

And irrationality means that you can see things and hear things that aren't really happening.

Like when you see your father (who is locked up in prison in another state) standing on a porch in the middle of the night.

And seeing things that aren't real is why it can be hard to breathe and why you feel like running as fast as your legs can carry you straight into a brick wall.

Or maybe into the ocean.

Over an edge.

Out of this town.

But you don't.

Instead, you realize that you have a big problem.

You ask for help.

Sam sat in front of the church in the dark of night. He couldn't go in. It was locked, but that didn't matter.

He spoke to the universe. He needed his world to be right again.

Sam felt his heart now beating somewhere inside his neck. He wiped his face, wet with sweat, and got to his feet.

By the time he got home, the sun was coming up, and he was exhausted and grateful for that.

*   *   *

Riddle couldn't get back to sleep for a long time after seeing the light in the window coming from the house next door.

He lay in the dark and listened to Jared's heavy breathing as he thought about the band of thieves who were robbing the Binghams.

In his mind he saw them taking the fancy spice set that was in the silver rack in the kitchen. He had admired those containers.

He imaged them scooping up the helpless tropical fish from the aquarium and putting them in clear plastic bags tied at the top in leaky knots.

Riddle shut his eyes and saw the bandits stuff ropes of jewelry into backpacks.

He could see them making off with the six-slice toaster that he so admired on the countertop next to the sink.

And then finally, just before the sun came up, he drifted off to sleep.

He had tried to stop it all.

But like so many times before, no one would listen to him.

* * *

It was after ten o'clock when Riddle opened his eyes to see the other bunk bed empty.

He pulled on clothes and went downstairs to find Jared eating a bowl of soggy cereal as he watched an old movie that he'd seen countless times about a bunch of kids playing soccer in a small town in Texas.

Jared looked up from the TV and said, "I thought you were gonna make pancakes. I waited for a while."

Riddle picked up the cat that was rubbing against his legs.

"I hope we don't get blamed, because I think robbers got into the neighbors' house last night."

Jared kept chewing. "How come you think that?"

Riddle was only looking at the cat. He was staring into her yellow eyes, which looked like liquid marbles.

"I know that I'm sort of blind, but I see things."

And Jared had to agree.

* * *

Jared called Beto, because there was no way he was going next door with just Riddle, even if he didn't really believe him.

Beto arrived right away, but he had to eat a bowl of cereal before he went over to check things out.

So it was almost eleven when they stood behind the house and discovered that the key was missing from under the brick.

They circled the yard in a three-headed cluster, peeking into windows for clues.

It wasn't until Beto tried the knob on the back door that they realized it was open.

Jared suddenly got very nervous. "Okay, let's go home and call my mom and dad. We could be messing up clues."

But Beto looked energized. "We locked this door. I remember. We locked it last night, and we put away the key!"

Riddle nodded. "We locked it. And now it's open, because someone got in."

Jared reached out and grabbed the back of Beto's T-shirt. "Don't go in. I mean it."

But Riddle was already in the kitchen, and Beto was right behind him.

* * *

Bitzie Evans cursed Emily Bell.

The shopkeeper wasn't happy that Emily didn't show up that morning to open the store. She didn't find out until she stopped by the Orange Tree after her weekly foot massage.

Bitzie held a new shipment of battery-powered candles in her arms and buzzed the back door of the store with the point of her elbow. And when Emily didn't answer, Bitzie angrily returned to her car, dug out her shop key from the snarl of crap in the compartment in between the two seats, and then set off the building alarm as she entered.

The place was still locked up from the night before.

She next checked her cell phone and the store phone, only to find she had no messages from the new salesgirl.

Bitzie punched in Emily's phone number, and when a message came on Bitzie felt her jaw tighten. She waited until the beep to say:

"Emily, this is Bitzie Evans from the Orange Tree. I just got here, and the store was locked up with the alarm still on. No excuse is good enough for not calling. I'm letting you go. That's just the way it is. No excuse will work with me."

Bitzie put the phone handset down hard into the cradle and turned on one of the battery-powered candles.

But the flameless flicker didn't make her feel any better.

* * *

Sam woke up, and the sun was high in the sky.

The first thing he did was reach for his phone and call Emily.

He was both relieved and upset that it went straight to voice mail. When he spoke into the phone, his voice cracked:

"Hey, Em. It's me. I had a rough night and needed to think some stuff through. So call me—okay? I'm going to class—but call me anyway. I love you. That's really what I want to say. I'll explain the other part when I see you."

Sam pressed End and felt better. He'd started the process.

He would explain what had happened with Destiny, and Emily would understand. He would make her understand.

Because she was the kind of person who understood everything.

Nothing had happened that would change anything between them.

Nothing.

33

You aren't lost until someone is trying to find you. And no one was looking for Emily Bell.

Beto and Riddle went inside the Binghams' house and discovered dirty dishes, empty alcohol bottles, and the upstairs drawers ransacked.

Jared, having a complete meltdown, waited outside.

The three boys then ran home, half out of their minds, and called Jared's parents, who called the police.

What followed was a police investigation.

The officers assumed that it would be difficult to determine what had been taken, but then Riddle sat down and started to draw precise pictures of everything that had been downstairs.

Beto and Jared looked over his shoulder as the pencil began to outline the kitchen. "You're like some kind of computer. How can you do that?" Beto was shocked. Riddle only continued to work on his detailed depiction of each room.

Suddenly it didn't matter as much that the Binghams couldn't be reached.

Debbie and Tim Bell both left work and came right home after receiving Jared's call. Debbie was worried that Riddle would be traumatized, but he appeared to be handling it better than anyone. He at least had a job to do. Everyone else could only huddle together and speculate.

It took an hour for the forensics expert to come and dust for fingerprints. But mostly what the guy thought he was getting were prints from the three boys.

It was assumed that Emily was at work at the Orange Tree, and Debbie, not wanting to add to the chaos, didn't alert her to any problem. And Sam had summer-school class, so they would both hear about the break-in at the end of the day.

*   *   *

During the course of the morning, Sam left Emily two messages on her cell phone and sent four texts and hadn't heard back.

That was strange, but he was feeling strange, so it didn't register that anything was really wrong with her.

Everything that was wrong was with him.

But when he got out of his morning class and she didn't answer her phone and still hadn't returned his text messages, a new feeling took hold.

Panic.

Sam phoned the Orange Tree and got a recorded greeting. So he got into his car and headed straight over to the shop.

*   *   *

Robb Ellis was standing on the sidewalk in front of Ferdinand's. He looked lost.

Sam pulled into a parking space and could see right away that the Orange Tree was closed. His gaze shifted to Robb, who didn't look happy. He made his way over to Sam's car. He leaned down and spoke through the open window.

"What's up?"

Sam was wondering the same thing. "I'm looking for Emily."

Robb nodded. "I'm looking for my car."

"Where's Destiny?"

"I'm not sure. She's not at work. I know that much."

They both were silent for what seemed like too long. Robb found himself thinking that if they were girls, a lot more information would have been exchanged.

Finally Sam asked, "Destiny doesn't answer her cell phone?"

Robb just shrugged. "She doesn't have one."

Sam nodded as if that were normal.

For seventeen years of his life, that was the case, but now that he'd been mainstreamed, rehabilitated, and brought into another world, the idea of not having a phone that you carried at all times seemed strange.

196

Sam finally offered up: "Emily isn't answering her phone. I haven't heard from her all morning, actually."

Now Robb nodded like that was normal, when he felt certain that it wasn't. He and Emily weren't even very friendly anymore, and she returned his calls right away. That's the kind of person she was.

Robb leaned back on his heels and decided to just come out with it. "We both had the day off from the restaurant. I slept in late, and when I woke up, Destiny and my car were gone."

Sam let this sink in.

He knew that Destiny was living in the motel. He'd dropped her there the night before.

A horrible feeling now gnawed hard in his gut.

He hadn't thought about Robb Ellis staying at the motel with Destiny, not that it mattered and not that it surprised him.

Did Robb know anything about what happened yesterday?

He didn't seem to. His sense of defeat looked completely unrelated to Sam, who finally said:

"Did she leave a note or anything?"

Robb sighed. "No. But all her clothes and her personal crap are in the motel. I sat around waiting for her for an hour. And then I walked over here, because I thought maybe she'd gone to the restaurant or something. But they haven't seen her."

Sam felt his heart race. He had to ask. "Do you think they're together?"

Robb gave it some thought. "I don't know. What do you think?"

Sam's mind went over the facts.

Two girls were missing.

Two girls who knew each other but didn't have much of a connection.

Unless you counted *him* as the connection.

And that was a sickening thought.

Destiny was messed up. Was it possible she'd done something to Emily? Would she try to hurt her?

Sam motioned to the passenger door. "Get in."

* * *

Clarence Border's name was in the news in Northern California, and his photo and a description were circulated to all agencies of law enforcement.

But Dennis Hauck, who was in charge of the First Alert program, fell down a flight of stairs on the afternoon that Clarence went missing from the Merced Medical Center bathroom.

Dennis was the California liaison to the other Pacific Northwest states. It was his job to make sure that interested parties were notified immediately when something like this happened.

Dennis fractured his ankle and spent two days away from his desk. Tammy Tolin was placed in charge while Dennis was out, and she flagged Clarence Border on her computer.

But when Dennis returned, his desktop files didn't sync

properly with what Tammy had used. Dennis had received an alert to upgrade his browser, but he had failed to do so.

And all of that meant he didn't see Tammy's notice. She assumed that he'd sent out electronic alerts to the Bell family in Oregon and that he'd also spoken to their local police department.

But that wasn't the case.

Dennis Hauck dropped the ball on four cases when his ankle failed him.

Only one of them mattered.

34

Destiny kept her distance, following the silver car but doing her best to be inconspicuous.

Her small fist slammed down into the surprisingly firm passenger seat of Robb Ellis's SUV.

If only I had a cell phone, I could call for help.

Or if she had better vision, she could get the license-plate number of the silver car and then pull over and tell someone what she'd seen.

But without a license plate, what would she say? And who would believe her?

To get that information, she had to be close. Really close. Because her eyesight was bad. Destiny had known she needed glasses since the blackboards at school started to go fuzzy. And that was back when she went to school, which was a long time ago.

Three blocks from Agate Street, the silver car turned onto Franklin, which had more traffic.

Two cars got ahead of her, but several miles down, she still had the silver car in view and watched as it made its way to the interstate on-ramp.

Sitting back on the crunched Kleenex box, Destiny didn't flinch.

She continued right on the freeway entrance and headed due north.

* * *

Outside the house Clarence had pushed the gun into the small of Emily's back as he said:

"You're the reason my boys turned against me."

She thought she would scream.

But she didn't. Fear was in charge. Terror took control.

And it was then that she began her out-of-body experience.

Because she was there but not there.

Her heart was beating and she was breathing, but it was impossible that this was happening to her.

She had never met this man. But she knew who he was.

She had first seen him in a picture that Robb Ellis had taken on his cell phone so many months ago when he'd followed Sam and Riddle out to the house on River Road.

And then she had seen a police photo when this monster was arrested.

She wasn't supposed to see that. But she had opened a file that her parents had printed out. It was paperwork for adopting Riddle. And it had been there.

This man was in prison.

He was never getting out.

But he was right here.

A second shadow-self repeated in an inner chant, *Make it stop. . . .*

But the monster, in an icy calm voice, had said to her:

"You and I are going on a drive. If you yell, or if you scream, I will shoot you. Right here, in your fancy brick drive-way, and I will shoot anyone who comes out of your house when they hear the shot fired. I will aim for their heads and I will take them all down with you. So now you have a choice. Now you can be an executioner."

And then he started to walk, the gun pushing against her side, and she moved with him.

Her legs felt funny, like they weren't there, and inside her head it was humming. Her ears rang.

Loud.

The humming was a buzz, like something electrical had snapped in her brain.

She didn't see anything. Not the dog barking in the front window. Not the kid riding by on his bicycle.

Not Robb Ellis's car parked on the street.

The only thing she could see now was walking next to her.

The monster.

And what sickened her was how she could make out Sam in the features of his face.

* * *

202

Inside the silver car, the buzzing got louder.

The monster drove down the street, not fast and not slow.

Just the speed limit. Cars whizzed past, and no one knew. None of them could see that something was deeply wrong inside the silver car.

He talked. It was to her, but it could have been to himself.

"When I come to a stop, you might think you can open the door and jump out. But if you open the door, I'll put my foot all the way down on the gas, and I'll drive straight into whatever is in front of me. It could be people in a crosswalk. It could be the gas tank of the car in front of me. Whatever it is, I'll do that. And I'll take it all down with us. How does that sound?"

She could hear him. She could understand him.

But it didn't make any sense.

He was locked up forever.

How did he end up at her back door?

She shut her eyes, and the buzzing in her head changed frequency. And then she opened her eyes, because she felt something inside her purse, which was still over her right shoulder and out of the monster's view.

It was vibrating.

Her cell phone. Someone was calling her.

Sam. She knew it was him.

But the phone did not ring, and then she remembered that the battery was low. She hadn't charged her phone at night. She hadn't followed any of her regular routine.

Emily closed her eyes again and willed Sam to somehow know that she needed help.

The vibrating stopped, and she watched, staring straight ahead out the windshield as he turned onto the on-ramp and merged into the northbound traffic.

And that was when he said, in a voice that was just an airless whisper, "Your parents stole my kids. Now I got you, babe."

35

Detective Sanderson drove an unmarked car, but like most unmarked police vehicles, it didn't take much attention to detail to notice that it wasn't ordinary.

The side-view and rearview mirrors were twice the regular size. The license plates didn't follow the regular state letter-number sequence. And the sheer nondescript nature of the boxy blue sedan in excellent condition seemed to shout that something was up.

Beto saw the car coming down the block and turned to Riddle. "The boss is here."

Two patrol cars were already parked at the curb, and neighbors from across the street were on the sidewalk talking to Tim Bell.

Three of the four officers were inside the Binghams' house. The remaining officer was outside with Debbie Bell.

The three kids had been instructed to stay inside the house, but they were on the Bells' porch. Riddle, sketch pad in his lap, was still drawing. They were part of this and they were not going to miss out on anything now.

As the unmarked car parked at a distance and Detective Sanderson got out, Riddle said: "I know him. He helped find me and Sam."

Beto was impressed. The idea that Riddle knew a detective was cool. The whole day was shaping up to be way more exciting than Beto would have ever imagined. He wondered if they would be in the news. He could see that happening.

Jared fidgeted, shifting his weight from side to side as he bit down on the inside of his cheek.

Beto's excitement couldn't be contained. "What if the bad guy is still in the neighborhood? What if he's watching us from someplace hidden? What if they find him now and there's a shoot-out? How cool would it be to see a real shoot-out!"

The expression on Jared's face said not cool at all.

Riddle's face was impossible to decipher.

All three boys held their breath as Detective Sanderson went into the house. He shot a look at the boys on the porch.

Riddle kept his eyes locked on the detective as he said, "He's in charge of secrets."

*   *   *

It wasn't a typical case of breaking and entering, because the person had spent time in the residence.

The intruder or intruders had left a dirty kitchen, an

unmade bed, wet towels (folded), and open drawers and cabinets.

The officers had no way of knowing that Clarence had packed the bulk of the casual wardrobe that Roland Bingham hadn't taken on his trip.

It was now in two duffel bags in the backseat of his car, along with their better pieces of silver, jewelry passed down from two generations of the family, the whiskey and scotch from the pantry, and most of their prescription medications.

The officers approached the crime in a procedural manner, even if it was unusual to have a criminal return to the freezer the unused portion of a bag of onion rings that he'd opened and broiled on a cookie sheet.

*   *   *

The lead officer, Jay Dooley, hadn't yet filed a report, so he was surprised to find Sanderson standing in the entry.

But the detective volunteered the explanation right away. "I know the people who called this in. The Bells."

Officer Dooley proceeded to go over the facts, which included that the residents were away on vacation and their home was being looked after by the neighbors. Specifically, three young boys.

The person who'd been inside had used the key.

Had someone been spying on the boys who were feeding the fish? Or had the boys told someone about the placement of the key?

It could have been the work of a transient, or teenagers, but it somehow didn't look that way.

Dooley lowered his voice when he made his final comment. "One of the kids isn't from the neighborhood. He goes to school with them but lives on the other side of the Ferry Street Bridge. His name's Roberto Moreno. They call him Beto. You might want to run a background check on his parents when you're in the station."

Sanderson looked at Officer Dooley's thick neck and made a note to run a background check instead on Dooley. He wondered if the guy had any prior incidents of racial discrimination.

Detective Darius Sanderson walked back to his car with a sour stomach. And it wasn't just because he was going to forgo lunch and work through the afternoon.

* * *

Moments later, Officer Dooley went to his car and filed his first report about the break-in.

While he waited for more information on fingerprints and other on-site DNA analysis (there had been samples taken from the bathroom and the bedroom where the intruder had slept), he concentrated on a ten-year-old named Roberto Moreno.

The kid knew something.

Dooley felt sure of it.

36

Destiny looked down at the gas gauge.

The needle showed that the tank was almost full. That was one thing about Robb Ellis: he may have had a patch of furlike hair at the base of his spine, but he also had a working credit card and he knew how to use it.

If she could ever get her life together enough to have her own car, she just knew she'd always be running on empty.

Up ahead the blue sky was turning milky white.

Destiny crinkled up her nose. Summer storms appeared from the mountains, and now it looked like she was driving into one.

No, she was following someone who was driving into one.

Now that she'd been on the road for nearly an hour, her concentration was flagging.

What if she'd gotten the whole thing wrong? What if the guy in the silver car up ahead going just three miles over the speed limit was Emily's uncle?

But why would an uncle put a gun in her back?

Maybe it wasn't a gun.

It certainly appeared to be a gun. And she'd seen weapons.

And why else would Emily's face have looked like a hunk of ice when she got in the car?

Destiny reassured herself that she was doing the right thing and kept her foot in the orange slipper pressed down on the gas pedal.

*   *   *

Emily dropped her right shoulder, forcing it to relax as she slowly worked to edge her purse off her body.

It took total concentration, but she was eventually able to get the soft leather strap to release, moving the bag down her arm against the door.

From there, she maneuvered her elbow to slip her right hand inside.

Her fingers angled through the leather opening and moved silently over the objects.

A hairbrush.

Lip gloss.

A key chain with a house key and a car key.

A ballpoint pen.

A mint candy wrapped in cellophane.

A hair scrunchie.

Her wallet.

A dime. A penny. A nickel. A dime.

A business card. She could feel the raised letters. It was from the optometrist. From when she and Sam took Riddle to get his new glasses.

Riddle. He had lived with this man for a decade. And so had Sam.

How had they survived?

Her fingers now ached as she thought of the two brothers.

And then, finally, her hand touched her cell phone.

Emily stared straight out the window as she pressed on the center dimple.

From there, she slid her index finger across the bottom. She had no way of knowing if it was on or what mode the phone would be in.

Or if the battery was so gone that nothing was now happening.

But she ran her fingertips over the bottom third of the glass screen, hoping that she was communicating something, anything, to the outside world.

*   *   *

Emily's best friend, Nora, officially hooked up with Rory the summer before junior year. Once Nora had a boyfriend, the two girls were no longer joined at the hip.

But they still spoke often, even in the summer. Emily was now with Sam. They both had jobs. They got used to not knowing exactly what the other person was doing.

That was a good thing. Really. Even if it made them both

sad to think that some of the closeness between them was now lost.

Nora was a lifeguard over the summer. Every ninety minutes she had a ten-minute break, when she and her lifeguard partner, Asher Luzatto, blew their whistles and cleared the pool.

Everyone was hauled out. The pool's sanitary levels were checked, and the lifeguards got a much-needed break. It was hard work doing nothing but sitting in a chair looking down into the bright light at splashing bodies.

Nora used the time to retreat to the shade of the small office, where she ate a snack and checked her messages.

Now, when she took out her phone, she saw a text sent from Emily. It said:

> Asdfghjkl;;zxcvbnm,./qwertyuiop[

Nora stared at the screen. There was a second message. It read:

> Sdfghjklasfghjklzxcvbnmm,./

Was it a joke? It didn't look funny.
And then, finally, a third text read:

> Poiuytrewq';lkjhgfdsa/.,mnbvcxz

Nora had a dull headache. Maybe it was spam. Because if it was some kind of complicated code, or even if it was an obvious puzzle, she wasn't getting it.

And so she sent back a simple reply:

?????

She then tossed the phone into her bag and went to get more sunscreen from the supply closet. She'd call Emily at the end of the day and see what was going on.

*   *   *

There were only two states of being.

In the first state, with the buzzing roaring in her head, Emily focused on studying what was exactly in front of her.

Literally.

The black molded plastic square, which covered the air vent of the dashboard, had a texture that looked like a miniature waffle. When the sunlight hit it in the right way, she could see a fine layer of dust. When the sunlight wasn't angled in that direction, the panel looked completely clean.

Emily worked to take the observation to the next step: dust particles were really just tiny pieces of dirt. Or plant pollen. Or human skin cells. She had studied dust in high school. In physics. No, maybe in some other class.

Would she ever go to high school again?

Freak out.

Back to buzzing state.

The floor mat was made of gray fibers. Clean, upright strands. Like gray synthetic grass.

The car seemed new. A new car with clean floor mats.

Alert. Previously unseen was a small stain near the back right edge of the mat. That could come out. It could be scrubbed. Maybe vacuumed first? Her parents liked clean cars.

Parents. Would she ever see her parents again?

Freak out.

The windshield had little yellowy streaks. Flecks of yellowy stuff. What were they? Droppings of some kind. From an animal?

There is an animal sitting behind the wheel.

A terrifying animal.

Freak out.

Back to the buzzing.

*　*　*

Second state of being: analyze an escape.

Make a plan.

Big-picture thinking.

The car is driving north on the freeway.

Maybe someone is looking for this car?

No one is looking for this car.

The vehicle is not speeding.

The other cars, the other people, so close but yet so far, cannot help.

But the vehicle will need gas at some point if he keeps driving.

Question: does he know where he's going? Does he have a plan?

He will have to stop the car for gas if he continues.

And what about eating?

Will he get hungry or thirsty?

And what about going to the bathroom? He will need to go to the bathroom.

When the car stops, what can be done?

If there are people around, how can they help?

Can her cell phone still send any kind of signal?

Why didn't she charge her phone?

Sam.

Because she saw Sam with Destiny.

Did she really see Sam with Destiny? Did she make that up in her head? Was it a bad dream? Was *this* a bad dream?

This is as real as it gets.

Were people looking for her right now?

Maybe her family knew that she was in trouble.

The dog knew. He was at the window. He saw.

No one would get her out of this. No one could help her. It was all on her.

A plan would involve running. She could run long distances because of soccer.

A plan would involve leaving a trail.

A signal.

A sign.

A plan is needed.

Dying is not part of any plan.

37

Clarence had eaten the leftover steak and onion rings from the night before when he'd woken up in the morning.

He'd had two cups of coffee. Both with a shot of bourbon.

Now, as he drove, his tongue worked to dislodge a piece of meat gristle stuck on the left side in his back molar. He was glad he'd had a good meal.

Breakfast was so important.

At his side the girl was quiet, and that was a good thing. She had the sense to just stare straight ahead, keep her mouth shut, and not ask a lot of dumb-ass questions.

He could see that her legs were trembling. Just slightly. And it wasn't cold, so that had to mean she was shaking from fear.

Sweet.

He'd killed a bird once, when he was small, by crushing it in his hands. It trembled when he held it. He remembered that now. And then he broke its neck, and it stopped shaking.

It was so peaceful and lifeless in the palm of his pale hand. It had been released from this world of pain.

He wanted the Bell family to remember him.

He would stop their daughter from shaking.

He could bring her to the peaceful place.

He just needed to figure out where and when.

*   *   *

Destiny worked on her plan.

She had to start with the license plate of the silver car. Once she had that information, she could get off the freeway and report the man and the gun and the girl. Hopefully, in no time, that would get a parade of highway-patrol cars powering after the bad guy.

But a few things were holding her back.

She made a list of potential obstacles as she drove.

1. She didn't have a valid driver's license. Would she get in trouble for that?
2. She had no ID, really. And she looked young. So young that people—authorities—might not even believe she was old enough to drive. What if they thought she was a runaway? That had happened before. In Tucson. But at that point she *was* a runaway. So maybe that didn't count.
3. She was driving Robb Ellis's car, and she hadn't asked, and now he might be mad. What if he'd

reported his car as stolen? He seemed pretty attached to his possessions. What if they hauled her away instead of going after the bad guy?

4. In order to see the license plate, she was going to have to pass the car. It was the only way she could get close enough. Why hadn't someone, anyone, thought to get her glasses?

Destiny squinted hard and then said out loud with fierce conviction, "I can do this."

She grabbed the rearview mirror and stared at herself as she said again: "I can do this."

She lingered on her own reflected image for a moment. She liked the way she looked—her hair was growing out in a good way. The dark roots now looked so intentional.

Then she reprimanded herself. *Focus.*

"I can..."

She put her foot down harder on the gas and pushed the mirror back in place as she said:

"...do this."

The black SUV pulled into the passing lane and in a matter of seconds had gained ground on the silver car.

As she got close, the rear of the Honda came into view more clearly, and she could see the license plate.

California
2KDZ7358

Destiny repeated it out loud:

"Two-K-D-Z-seven-three-five-eight."

The silver car with the man with the orange-colored hair was now right alongside her. Destiny quickly glanced over and could see he was staring straight ahead, both hands on the steering wheel.

The edge of Emily was visible in the passenger's seat and she, too, was looking straight out the windshield.

They both looked like mannequins. Not real.

Destiny traveled ten seconds ahead, counting the time out loud, and then slid back over into the right lane.

*   *   *

Emily barely blinked.

The electrical buzzing sound in her head had transported her. She was no longer in the car. She was walking along the Oregon coast, and the wind, as always, was blowing hard. The waves, in a dozen shades of gray, were crashing in sets of threes, sending a cold, salty spray high into the air.

Sam was with her. They were walking together. He wrapped his arm around her and held her close. And then, because they were alone, just the two of them, he sang to her. He could play his guitar in front of anyone. But singing was something different. It was only for her.

And then, right in the middle of the make-believe ocean walk, she saw Bobby/Robb Ellis's black car pull over from the left lane.

Bobby's SUV was in front of her.

The buzzing was now screaming in her ears.

What she saw had to be a mistake.

They'd been driving for a long time, and they were in the middle of nowhere, as far as she could tell.

But when she looked straight out the windshield, she could see the SUV, and she knew that car. She had ridden in that car countless times.

She knew the sticker in the back window for the country club. It had been put on just a little bit crooked. And she recognized the license-plate holder, which said *Max Miller's Ford*.

Max Miller's Ford was, of course, where the Ellis family had bought the car. Max Miller Jr. and his sister, Kyle, owned the place, since they'd inherited it from their father. And both Max and Kyle had kids. Maggie and Harper and Ryan and Fish Miller all went to school with Emily.

How many new black SUVs had little crooked stickers on the back for a country club?

How many had license-plate holders that said *Max Miller's Ford*?

Emily's heart was pounding so hard, she thought it was going to explode right out of her chest.

And then she watched, helpless to do anything, as Robb Ellis's SUV turned off the freeway at the next exit and disappeared up an incline.

But it didn't vanish before she had a chance to catch sight of the driver.

And that's when she saw Destiny.

* * *

Everything was jumbling up in Destiny's mind.

Why had she counted the ten seconds out loud? It ruined everything.

She struggled to repeat what she'd seen: *2KDZ7358.* But it was morphing now. She was too agitated, and she was losing the sequence.

The *2KD* had turned to *2KC,* and the *Z* was moving into a *J.*

She had the *7,* but she couldn't hold the *3* or the *8.*

She should have written it down, but she didn't have a pen. She didn't have paper.

And she was freaking out now.

Why hadn't she added up the numbers or turned them into something with meaning? Well, she didn't, and suddenly she had *2KCJ* and just the *7.*

And now she really didn't think it was *KCJ.*

She felt certain really only about the first *2.* And the *K.*

And the rest was lost.

Junk.

No wonder she'd hated math class. Numbers were just impossible for her unless they were on a price tag.

And then the highway exit also turned into a betrayal.

It dumped out onto a road, and there was not a gas station or a restaurant or a house or anything.

There was no one to help.

She stared out the windshield and saw only a road that

went up and over the interstate. And so she drove right through the stop sign at the top of the incline and straight across the blacktop and down the ramp back onto the freeway.

Destiny shouted out loud to the universe: "Bollocks!"

She had worked in a bar for six weeks by Mount Shasta, and there had been a bartender there named Ollie and he was from England and when things didn't go the right way he'd always yell, "Bollocks."

She wasn't sure what it meant, but she knew that her first attempt at going for help was a complete failure.

Destiny accelerated until she saw the silver car up ahead again.

And she eased up on the gas, relieved to just be the one to follow.

38

Sam and Robb sat in Sam's car outside Diane's Burger Heaven.

They were both worried, but they were also hungry, and so the decision was made to get cheeseburgers, fries, and chocolate milk shakes.

They were going to eat and make a plan, but instead they sat in Sam's car chewing in total silence.

Sam didn't know if he should tell Robb Ellis about his encounter with Destiny.

Could Destiny have told Emily about last night?

Was it possible the two girls were together?

Would Destiny have tried to hurt Emily?

And if he was really worried about the issue of Emily's personal safety, shouldn't he call her parents?

Robb, eating his cheeseburger in the passenger's seat, had his own list of questions.

How he was going to explain to his parents that he'd basically been lying about sleeping at Rory's?

Because, if Destiny Verbeck stole his car, which was a distinct possibility, who knew what else she might have up her sleeve that belonged to him?

Robb wondered if she'd gone to San Diego. Hadn't she said something about wanting to see panda bear babies that were just born? She'd said *something* about panda bears; he felt certain of that. The trouble was that she talked so much. He didn't actually hear half of what came out of her mouth.

And she got irritable easily. Or at least it felt that way. Especially since a lot of her irritation was directed at him.

And now this.

Robb glanced over at Sam. He looked a million miles away. Then Sam suddenly said, "I should tell you something...."

Sam put the rest of his cheeseburger into the greasy sack and obsessed over making the now-trash bag as small as possible as he continued. "Destiny showed up at my summer school class yesterday.... I ended up driving her back to the motel."

Robb raised an eyebrow. For him, this was a big reaction. But he didn't say anything.

"In the car she was...sort of...all over me. I told her I had a girlfriend, which of course she already knew. But she didn't seem too happy about that."

Robb kept eating his French fries. Dipping each one deeper into the ketchup as if he were being paid for how well he coated the end of the potato piece. It looked like he wasn't even listening now.

225

But he was listening. Totally listening. And he heard a voice inside his head screaming, *Why does this stuff always happen?*

Why do chicks turn against me?

He tried.

He really tried.

He bought Destiny the pink gemstone hairclips she liked so much at Rite Aid.

He held the door for her when they walked into buildings, like his parents had always told him to do.

He told her how pretty she was, and he brushed his teeth before he kissed her. And he used dental floss.

It was just so unfair.

Okay, so she didn't like him that much. So what?

She was just a short girl with bizarro clothes who smelled like candy corn, which was weird, because he never saw her even eat a single kernel of candy corn. And it was a fact that he never trusted her.

Not really, anyway.

Sam could have her.

Robb glanced over, and the expression on Sam's face said he really didn't want her. But he looked guilty, so maybe he did want her a little bit.

That wasn't even the point.

Robb needed to stick to the real problem, which was that his car was missing.

He tried to keep his voice from getting all high and squeaky, because it sometimes could be that way when he was upset. "I'm not that into Destiny. I'm really just worried, you know, about my car right now."

226

Sam replied, "Okay, well, I *am* worried about Emily. And maybe the car is connected. So what do you think we should do?"

With the disclosure about Destiny now behind them, they were finding more stable ground.

Robb Ellis knew about law enforcement and stolen property. "The first thing you always do is report the crime."

And then it was like a lightbulb came on. For the first time that day, Robb Ellis felt like his world wasn't collapsing. He wasn't trapped in an airless plastic container.

"I've got OnBoard. My car. It's got that service."

"What's OnBoard?"

Robb erupted. "It's a security system—you pay for it. You know, remote diagnostics. It records everything, turn by turn. It's tied into the car's phone system. It uses the GPS technology. It can even slow the car down. It's remote interface."

Sam didn't understand, but it was obvious to him that whatever Robb was saying was a big deal.

"So you mean we call the police and we report your car missing, and they can find it?"

Robb shook his head. "We don't need the police. My mom's a detective. I just call the service like I'm someone from her office. She's hooked up. There's a code I give the OnBoard operator, and then they'll give me a location. You and I can take care of this ourselves."

Sam knew that he had a lot to learn about the real world, but this was a revelation.

39

The boys stayed on the porch until the police cars and the neighbors were long gone. They hadn't done anything wrong, but they still felt partly responsible for the break-in.

Debbie Bell needed to return to her shift at the hospital. Tim Bell would stay at home and work from his basement studio. He'd keep an eye on the boys.

They sat on the edges of the porch railing, and Riddle continued to draw. He had done a "before" picture of the rooms downstairs. Now he was working on the "after." The "after" picture had a broiler pan in the sink and the dishes on the counter.

It was a perfect replica of the crime scene.

Beto watched from over his shoulder. "How do you remember all that stuff?"

Riddle just shrugged. "I take a picture in my mind, and then I can just look at that."

Beto glanced over at Jared. "There has to be a way that we can harness your power. I feel like we could make a lot of money in Las Vegas or get on a TV show."

Riddle looked across the yard at the Binghams' house. "I want to go back over there."

Beto seemed intrigued, but Jared piped up: "They told us not to. The police said it was a crime scene."

As Jared and Beto started to argue about what that meant, Riddle put his drawing pad down. "I'll be right back."

Riddle went to the kitchen. He'd seen the police officers hand Debbie Bell a piece of paper. He found what he was looking for on the counter. There were three telephone numbers with a single sentence. Riddle stared down and did his best to read the words.

Call Officer Dooley with questions or concerns.

At first it confused him. Why was a *q* just not a *k*? And why was a *c* sometimes an *s*?

But he got it. He read the line. He understood. Riddle felt the power of that comprehension surge through his body like an electric current.

And then underneath the sentence he saw in smaller print:

Roberto Moreno

He wondered why the officer had written that down. Riddle put the paper back on the counter and headed to the porch.

* * *

229

Riddle suddenly wanted to go to Beto's house. He didn't do much to explain why, but he had a feeling, and that was enough. Jared didn't want to be left behind. "We've got to stick together. The burglar is still out there."

Beto picked up his skateboard. "If he comes to our house, he'll have to deal with my grandpa. He's got bad knees, but he sleeps with a baseball bat by the bed. I wouldn't want to mess with him."

Beto's family lived across town, and it took a while to get there because Riddle was a terrible skateboarder.

As they approached the small wooden house, the three boys were surprised to see a police car parked out front. Beto's sunny disposition evaporated.

"What's going on?"

Jared grabbed Beto's sleeve. "Do you think the robber got into your place, too?"

The boys wordlessly headed across the thin strip of front lawn.

A sprinkler at the end of a gray hose was responsible for keeping the center of the grass green, but the perimeter was dry and turning brown.

Riddle stopped to look, mumbling to Jared, "They don't have automatic irrigation. I like the pattern the sprinkler made."

Jared didn't say anything, but he wondered how Riddle noticed so much small stuff and why he cared.

* * *

Inside, the boys immediately recognized the two officers. They had been at the Binghams'.

The police were on the couch, but on the edge of the cushions as if at any moment they might spring into some kind of action. Beto's grandfather, Felipe, was seated in a lounge chair.

"What's going on?" Beto interrupted.

Before Felipe could answer, the taller of the two men stood up. "We had a few questions to ask Mr. Moreno."

Beto looked at the officers. "What kind of questions?"

Beto's grandfather's voice sounded tired. "You boys go out back. I'm in the middle of something here."

But Beto didn't move. He was only ten years old, but suddenly he had the demeanor of a world-weary adult. He took a step toward the officers.

"He doesn't have to answer anything. And you don't have the right to even be here in our house without some kind of warrant."

Jared and Riddle both stared. This was a side of Beto that they'd never seen. The happy-go-lucky kid was now as serious as a heart attack.

The policemen exchanged a look.

Beto's grandfather reached out and put his hand on Beto's shoulder. "*Mijo*, I've got this covered. Wait in the yard."

But Beto wasn't going to wait anywhere. His gaze returned to the police officers. "Why are you here? You think I told someone where that key was, don't you? You think I gave someone that key?"

The room was quiet. Riddle looked from his friends to the law enforcement.

Beto seemed to have nailed it, because they weren't denying anything.

And then suddenly Riddle found himself saying: "I think someone was watching the house. They saw us take the key and put it back."

The larger of the two officers turned to Riddle. "Why would someone be watching you?"

Riddle answered: "That's what crooks do."

It was the most obvious statement in the world, but coming out of Riddle's mouth in such a matter-of-fact way, it sounded profound.

Riddle continued. "You could see us from the street when we got the key."

The two police officers didn't acknowledge what he'd said.

Riddle's head tilted to the side as he continued. "You should be asking who would want to come to the house? Why would someone be watching the neighbors? Or watching us? Who would that person be?"

And then Riddle suddenly felt sick to his stomach, because he was a person who saw the small things. All the details. And he hadn't realized something until now.

It had been in the picture he'd drawn.

The large, empty box of saltine crackers. It had been left on the counter in the Binghams' kitchen.

There were four sleeves of crackers in a box. And forty crackers in each sleeve.

How many people ate their way through that many saltines?

40

Sam drove Robb Ellis to his parents' office building. It was midday, and his father's car was gone from the parking lot, so Robb had Sam take the open space. They'd just be in and out.

Upstairs, Robb stood awkwardly in the doorway looking at Merle, who did the billing for his mother's private investigation firm.

Robb called out, with just a little too much exuberance, "Hey, Merle."

The accountant was always nice, but deep down, not really that deep, Robb felt like she hated him.

Merle quickly hit one of the letters on her keyboard, and the screen switched from a photo album of Africa to a spreadsheet. "Hey, Bobby."

He tried not to be irritated, because Merle knew that he'd changed from Bobby Ellis to Robb Ellis, but she couldn't accept that. She was acting like she was family, because his family couldn't be retrained in the name department.

Robb made a mental note to tell his mom that Merle was looking at her vacation pictures instead of balancing the books. He then stepped deeper inside the room, revealing Sam, who was behind him.

"This is Sam," Robb muttered.

He would have offered more of an explanation, but Merle was smiling at Sam for real, not the fake way she smiled whenever he came in, and it totally bugged him.

Sam tried to look at ease. But even feeling panicked, he seemed more grounded than Robb Ellis, who was hardwired to be a nerve center.

"Nice to meet you!" Merle's hands went to her thick mop of hair, and she ran her fingers through it like something sticky just dropped from the ceiling tiles. "Merle Kleingrove."

Robb hadn't seen this totally embarrassing side of the accountant before. He needed to stop it. "Sam and I are going to just hang out in the conference room."

Merle nodded as if that were normal, even though Robb had never in his life brought someone to the office and gone into the conference room. The conference room was for clients.

Did Merle think Sam was some kind of client?

Merle stood up, revealing her stretchy aqua exercise pants. She'd been warned about that. Robb's mother said there was nothing more unprofessional than people wearing exercise clothing in the workplace. "I can bring you donuts or coffee or—"

But Robb was already leading Sam down the hallway and no longer giving her the time of day.

*   *   *

Robb asked to speak to a level-two OnBoard technician.

It was critical, as he explained to Sam with his hand over the mouthpiece, to jump over the first-level people in any organization. And in the case of OnBoard, the first-level workers were really nothing more than phone operators.

Robb knew what he was doing, and in a matter of moments he had given the new person on the line a code, which indicated he had some kind of law-enforcement clearance.

He was now waiting for the response.

Sam sat across from him, sending Emily one more text.

He kept hoping that she'd just answer her phone or send him a message, and all of this would be over.

It was more than likely that everything was going to be completely explainable, like Emily and Destiny had bumped into each other and decided to take a walk or get a smoothie, and then they had a flat tire or found a dog running loose.

Stuff like that happened. Not to him, but to everyone else.

To him, someone missing was really gone.

Because they had been taken.

*   *   *

Robb gestured to Sam that he needed paper and something to write with.

There was a yellow legal pad on a corner table, and Sam

jumped for it just in time for Robb to say, "Milepost 182. Route 97."

Sam watched, feeling powerless, as Robb continued. "Thank you. Yes. Will do."

And then he hung up the phone, and suddenly his entire amped-up, boss-man attitude was gone. He tripped over his words as he said, "My car is over one hundred miles away from here!"

"Do you think it was stolen?"

"You mean by Destiny?"

"I don't know...."

"Well, it was stolen by somebody!"

Robb got to his feet. Destiny was his girlfriend. He'd spent the night at the motel. He'd paid for the place. He'd trusted her.

And now he realized that he'd been shot down by friendly fire. She had betrayed him.

He was learning the cruelest lesson of all this summer.

The worst enemy was always within the trusted circle.

* * *

Sometimes knowing the right people worked against you.

The city parking enforcement worker was writing up a ticket when the boys went out the back door. Robb Ellis's parents made sure that the two spaces behind their building, which were, of course, on their property, were only for them.

Sam was driving the Bells' third car, which was assumed to be a violator.

Robb took the ticket off the windshield. If he weren't so upset about his stolen SUV, he might have tried to talk his way out of the situation.

But not now. He grumbled in Sam's direction. "I'll pay for it. I told you to park here."

*   *   *

According to the Internet search, it was 102 miles to La Pine. They were, as Robb Ellis said, "in pursuit." And because of that, Robb persuaded Sam to let him drive.

Sam was okay with that, because he had no intention of speeding, and Robb clearly didn't have a problem right now with going over limits.

They pulled out of the alley behind the office, already moving too fast. As they merged onto the highway, eleven blocks later, Sam questioned whether they were doing the right thing. The speed limit was fifty-five in this section of the roadway, and he was already going seventy-five.

But Robb seemed to have an answer for everything. When Sam said that the last thing they needed was a speeding ticket, Robb assured him that he had an "in" with the state troopers.

Sam wasn't so sure.

But everything now was about Emily.

She was in danger.

He had no idea exactly how, but he was pretty sure it was connected to him.

41

He would shoot her.

Not in the car, because Clarence wasn't about to clean up the mess. The best thing would be to put a bullet through her head in the woods. Maybe with a river or a lake nearby.

If he tied a brick or a rock around her body, and if she stayed under long enough, he could get lucky and no one would ever find her.

He liked that.

If she was out in the wild long enough, she'd be scavenged by animals. A coyote or a red fox or two would do a good job on her carcass. Especially in the summertime.

Just the hint of a smile appeared on his face as he thought of the family, for the rest of their lives, waiting for her to come home.

Now that was torture.

Every ring of a phone or knock on the door could be a flicker of hope.

He hated that word.

Hope.

It was so overused and so full of crap.

It rhymed with *dope* and *grope* and *rope*. All better words, because those things were real.

They had pain.

*　*　*

Emily didn't know anymore if it was just in her mind.

Bobby Ellis's car.

Destiny behind the wheel.

That just didn't make sense.

But what did right now?

The buzzing had gotten so loud that she was hearing things *and* seeing things.

Her eyes were dry. She realized that she'd been staring straight ahead, barely moving, for so long that it was difficult to even blink.

She forced herself back into her own body.

And realized that breathing was as important as anything right now.

*　*　*

On the east side of the interstate, up ahead, Clarence saw a sign.

It indicated that there was a rest stop in five miles. But a highway department overlay that was made out of some kind of netting said *Closed for Maintenance.*

He had to go to the bathroom. He was getting hungry. And his hacked-off foot hurt. He needed to pop more of the pain pills that he'd pocketed from the medicine chest in the house with the fish tank.

But most of all, he needed to get rid of her.

She was limiting his options.

She needed to be "closed for maintenance."

But at a rest stop?

So public. Too many variables.

He could just pull over at a random exit and get off and find some place that was isolated.

But thinking it through, he realized it didn't need to be remote enough for him to shoot her. Just enough out of the way to get her into the trunk.

He'd have done that to begin with, except that if anyone had spotted a teenage girl climbing into the trunk of a car in such a nice neighborhood, they'd think it was strange.

But now, in the middle of nowhere, he could lock her in the back and take his time deciding where to pull the trigger. If she somehow suffocated while trapped there—all the better.

A closed rest stop could be just what he was looking for.

He glanced over at the passenger seat.

She was different now than before. She was sitting up straighter and paying attention in a new way.

Had she seen something that he'd missed?

Not likely.

He took in a lot more detail than most people.

So he felt certain that she'd be no match for him in that arena.

*　*　*

Destiny saw the sign for the rest stop, but she didn't think anything of it because there was some kind of plastic covering that said it was closed.

Was he turning off?

Now this was a problem.

Should she follow?

She didn't have time to weigh her options.

She just put her foot on the brake.

He's going to a rest stop.

But the sign said it's closed.

There are cones but not a barrier.

And he's going around them.

What does he know about this place?

Has he traveled this far to come here? Is someone waiting for him there?

*　*　*

They were pulling off the highway.

Did he have to use a bathroom?

She did. Would he let Emily do that?

If he didn't, would she just pee right there in the car seat?

Would he kill her in a closed rest stop?

Tall trees made the area impossible to see from the highway.

It was private.

And it was officially closed.

It was now the scariest thing she had ever seen.

He was slowing down.

Up ahead, across the empty parking lot, was a single big rig truck.

On a grassy area nearby was a brown-painted cinder-block structure.

Bathrooms.

Emily did a mental inventory:

Three metal drum trash cans.

Two picnic tables.

A carved map of Oregon on a wooden sign.

A list of rules on the side of the cinder-block bathroom building.

A large pile of sand.

A large pile of gravel.

A pyramid of new cinder blocks.

A stack of blinking highway marker signs.

A blue tarp next to the signs.

That was it. No highway workers. No state vehicles.

From a distance it didn't look like anyone was in the big rig. So was the driver inside the bathrooms?

Would he come out?

Could he save her?

As they got closer, she saw a wooden barrier in front of the entrance to the cinder-block building. A sign read: *Bathrooms Not in Service.*

Emily curled and uncurled her toes.

An empty parking lot.

A closed cinder-block bathroom building.

A big rig.

And the Monster.

*   *   *

Clarence drove past the obvious parking spots, the ones right in front of the cinder-block bathroom structure. He maneuvered to the edge of the lot to a place in the corner under the cover of a row of large pine trees.

The area screamed privacy.

If the big rig hadn't been there, he could just take the girl out into the woods right there and finish her.

He couldn't see a driver in the truck, but still. He wouldn't risk it.

He slid the Honda into the parking space, and then just before he could even cut the engine, another car came into view. A black SUV appeared, coming around the curve into the rest stop.

What was that about?

Couldn't the driver read the sign?

This rest stop is closed!

What was wrong with people?

Clarence stared at the SUV. It was moving slowly.

Too slowly, he thought. Maybe engine trouble. The glare on the windshield of the SUV made it impossible to see the person behind the wheel.

Clarence kept the motor running.

Wait and see.

See and wait.

He didn't want any extra trouble.

42

As they traveled down the highway, Sam silently made deals with the universe. He swore that if Emily was okay, he'd devote his life to helping people.

Sick people.

Poor people.

All kinds of needy people.

He would be a priest or a minister or whatever was the highest calling.

If it meant giving up music, he'd do that.

He'd move away. He'd leave everything behind. He would sacrifice anything to have Emily be all right. He'd give his own life.

Sam's lips moved as he spoke the words out loud: "Just let her be all right."

This day, he thought, needed to end with the discovery of Emily reading a book in a library. She'd fallen asleep. Her cell phone was off. There had been no reason to panic.

There would be no connection to Robb's car or Destiny.

It would all be a big mix-up.

But he said over and over again to himself:

Just let her be okay.

* * *

Robb Ellis was staring at Rabbit Ears.

That was what the strange rock formation was called.

He was in the driver's seat, looking out the window at the two rocks that jutted up from the sea of pine trees.

And then suddenly there was a siren behind them with swirling lights and a voice commanding that the car pull over.

Robb put his foot on the brake. "If we were in *my* car, this wouldn't be happening. I have a radar detector."

Sam looked at him. "We're trying to find your car. So if we were in your car, of course this wouldn't be happening."

Robb exhaled as he shut his eyes, mumbling to himself: "Man up."

Moments later the state trooper had his head in the window. "I just need your license."

The ticket was for going eighty-seven miles an hour in a fifty-five-mile-an-hour zone.

* * *

After the ticket they didn't get far, because Robb had to take a leak. He pulled Sam's car over to an area along the roadway.

Standing there, doing his business under the heavy canopy of old-growth trees, Robb suddenly heard high-pitched squeaking.

He realized that the sound was above him. But just as he raised his head, something fell from a treetop nest.

And it landed right in his face.

The baby bat, nocturnal, only two weeks old, was not yet able to do more than eat and sleep and squeak. The little animal had been positioned poorly in the nest, and gravity had won the only battle being waged.

But when the baby bat hit Robb's head, his freak-out was so extreme that he took off in a sprint, lost his balance, and slid on moss.

His ankles, he immediately realized when he went down, were always wobbly.

*   *   *

Sam waited in the car for ten minutes, which felt like an hour, before he opened the door to see what was taking Robb so long.

Was he doing more than just taking a leak?

The idea of finding Robb Ellis squatting somewhere out in the ferns was more than disturbing.

Maybe Robb had encountered a bear or a wolf or a mountain lion. Or maybe he'd stepped into an old, rusty hunting trap and was now thinking of gnawing off his own limb.

Whatever he was doing, it was keeping them from heading after Robb's car and possibly finding Emily.

And nothing else mattered but her disappearance, his bad behavior, and the threat that was a girl named Destiny.

*   *   *

It was incredibly quiet when Sam opened the car door and started down the slope into the dense woods.

The undergrowth of moss and ferns made a kind of carpet, and Sam knew how to spot where it had been disturbed.

He found the baby bat before he found Robb. It lay on its back at the base of a towering tree. It was tiny, with immature, limp wings that were translucent even in the half-light.

The little baby's perfect body was so fragile that Sam found himself transfixed at the sight.

Only moments before, the small animal had been alive. Sam forced himself not to connect what he was seeing to Emily.

The world wasn't a big web where everything had a reason for being or meaning in a greater context.

Bats carried rabies.

Clarence had always warned about that.

Sam felt the panic full on. It gripped his throat and made breathing difficult. His father should be the last of his problems right now. The man was locked up and had nothing to do with what was now happening, and any thought of him was just ridiculous.

And then he heard a voice: "I'm over here."

Only forty feet away, crumpled in a hole, was Robb Ellis. Sam dropped to his knees. "What happened?"

Robb tried to pull himself to a seated position, but he was still dazed. "I'm not sure."

"Just take a breath. Take it easy...." Sam nodded, adding, "Did you see a bat?"

It was all coming back to Robb now.

"Yeah. It flew down and hit me in the face. I freaked out."

Sam shrugged. "Stuff happens."

Robb started to get up. "You must think I'm the biggest dork."

"Not really."

Robb was suddenly very coherent. "I am. That's the truth."

Sam helped him to his feet. "Maybe you think too much about what everyone else is thinking about you."

Robb considered the possibility. "You say the most simple things, and somehow it's like you're a prophet."

Sam shook his head. "Only to you, Robb."

"Call me Bobby. That's my name." He started up the incline to the road. "The Robb thing is so pretentious."

Sam raised an eyebrow. "I'm not really sure what *pretentious* means."

Robb/Bobby shook his head. "Of course not. That's perfect."

43

Destiny spotted the silver car across the way, idling in the corner of the parking lot. There was a big rig parked at an angle at a distance from the bathrooms.

Clouds had rolled down from the mountains, and the sky was a milky-white blanket above, which made no shadows below.

Only a slight breeze stirred the air.

It was quiet. And calm.

She needed to be the same way.

She said it out loud: "Look normal."

She should do that *now*.

And so Destiny swung Robb Ellis's SUV into the spot closest to the cinder-block bathrooms.

Isn't that what most people would do, even if they went into a closed rest stop? Wouldn't they be coming in to use the bathroom?

Should she get out? Should she go around the wood barricade and into the cinder-block building?

As Destiny deliberated, she could see the copper-haired man at the wheel of the silver car. And the edge of Emily.

But the man's head was now twisting around in her direction.

And he was looking right at her.

*   *   *

Emily stared forward.

But she watched by looking in the side-view mirror as the door of Robb Ellis's SUV opened and Destiny Verbeck became visible.

Her yellow-and-blue sundress and snug orange shoes made her look dainty from a distance. Even fragile.

She was real. So it can't be a coincidence. She has to be following us.

Because didn't she just get off the highway at a closed rest stop?

Next to her the Monster spoke. "Some kid musta stole her parents' car."

He seemed to admire this. Not condemn it.

His full attention was now locked on Destiny.

*   *   *

K.B. Walton was a trucker who'd driven for forty-one years.

He was a long-haul man, traversing the country the way other people make trips to their local grocery store.

As K.B. saw it, he was a modern-day cowboy. He moved stuff across wide-open spaces. And he did it alone, for the most part, communing in his own way with nature and the elements.

While he was out there battling the wind and the rain and the loneliness of the open road, he disappeared into his own thoughts, which might have been boring and dull to other people, but to K.B., they were what brought him comfort and peace.

He sang as he drove, mostly songs that he made up. His favorite creations had a country-and-western feel, and the one he was working on now was titled "How Many Scented Soaps Can a Single Man Own?"

During the course of his four decades of hauling everything from rawhide strips to cases of multicolored Italian gum balls, he'd upgraded so that he now drove a rig that had a sleeper unit complete with a mini-fridge, a toilet/shower combo, and a bed that swung down right on top of a small booth that was otherwise a tabletop.

The road had given K.B. something else besides a catalog of confessional songs, a way to pay his bills, and an escape from his boozer wife and two now-grown daughters.

It had also given him hemorrhoids, high blood pressure, and peripheral neuropathy.

The neuropathy was now his real problem. It caused tingling in his hands and his feet. And it played tricks when he least expected it, turning whole parts of his body numb and achy and cold.

With K.B.'s disability, his reaction time was slowing.

And that could be a problem for someone behind the controls of eighteen wheels of heavy machinery.

His solution was to keep his troubles to himself. He was an independent operator, so he didn't have a boss. If he got his loads delivered on time, no one cared how the stuff got there, or if the person responsible had been numb on the left side of his body for 2,856 miles.

But that morning, as he chugged up Route 97 in central Oregon, it was all catching up to him.

His left hand, his wrist, and his left elbow were immobile. His left shoulder felt like it had been frozen solid. And the tingling was spreading.

The rest stop was officially closed, but K.B. Walton realized that he had no choice but to pull over to see if he could shake the feeling of a hundred tiny bee stings in his left foot.

He parked his rig in the vacant lot, climbed into the living cubicle behind the driver's seat, and put down the fold-out bunk bed.

He drank a fair amount of whiskey from the bottle he kept in the box above the shower/toilet stall, and he fell asleep.

*   *   *

Destiny held the keys to Robb Ellis's car firmly in hand as she went around the wooden barricade and into the cinder-block building.

She realized that she was shaking.

She gripped the keys tighter and tried to focus on her surroundings.

The space was dissected into two parts by an open corridor that was covered by a green corrugated-plastic roof.

You could go left to the men's section or to the right to the women's part. Or you could walk straight, and you'd end up out the back.

There were two entrances and exits. That made Destiny feel better and worse at the same time.

Public bathrooms always smelled the same to her. Weird and closed in and creepy.

Now every detail of the place jumped out at her.

There were brown paper towels scattered on the cement floor, and someone had spray painted graffiti on the gray cinder-block wall. It read:

BAD SPELLERS OF THE WORLD, UNTIE!

Instead of going into the women's side, Destiny silently moved down the center corridor, emerging out the back of the building.

A metal drinking fountain was attached to the wall. Someone had written in black Magic Marker next to the on/off handle:

Please Wiggle Handel

Written below this, in a different color marker, was:

If I do, will it wiggle Bach?

Destiny had no idea what that meant.

She looked down at her hand and realized that she was clutching Robb's car keys so tightly that what must have been his house key had sliced a cut into her palm.

She forced herself to loosen her grip, and after a few deep breaths she moved to the corner of the building, where she peeked out at the parking lot.

The big rig looked abandoned.

But she could still see the orange-haired man and Emily in the silver car.

*   *   *

Clarence ran his fingers through his hair, which suddenly felt greasy.

Being clean was very important to him.

Maybe it was the heat, or maybe it was the buzz he got from breaking the law.

He was jacked up, that was for sure.

If the midget hadn't shown up in the SUV, he'd have popped the girl by now.

His gun was just waiting to fire.

So what was taking the troll-baby so long? He saw her go around the wooden barrier and into the bathroom. He could imagine her now, sitting on a toilet, taking her sweet time. Did her feet even reach the ground?

And he had to go, too, damn it.

Clarence, temper rising, shifted abruptly out of park and

into reverse. He stepped on the gas and made a loop, backing up so that the hood of the car was now facing the cinderblock building. This gave him a better view of the bathroom, and the trunk of the Honda was facing the other direction.

It was now hidden.

If the SUV elf didn't come out in the next sixty seconds, he'd go to plan B.

Or even plan C.

*   *   *

Emily could feel him growing more and more anxious. His fingers were strumming, and his right leg twitched. Little kicks forward at nothing but air.

So she tried hard to stay still.

To be invisible.

To not provoke him.

Everything that Sam had ever told her about the man came back to her now. He heard voices. They told him what to do. He made decisions. Sudden. Irrational.

The boys had been afraid of him. That's most of what she could remember: fear of his very being. How had Sam lived under this kind of tyranny for so many years?

Emily's love for Sam and Riddle made her now feel as if she would explode. She had never experienced such a surge of emotion.

She understood suddenly that the two boys were some kind of miracle. They had survived this.

And then a voice, *his* voice, spoke.

"We're going to get out of the car. I'll come around and open your door. And then we're going behind the car. If you run, if you even turn the wrong way, I'll shoot you. Your choice."

Emily knew how to do manipulation techniques to solve derivations in calculus using a graphing calculator. She knew how to conjugate Spanish language verbs in six tenses. But she had not been taught about psychopaths.

She struggled to use her ability to feel what he was feeling. And right now she knew he was a bundle of frustration.

He was ready to blow up.

Emily suddenly shifted to Destiny. She tried to imagine what was happening in that bathroom.

Forget how she got in Bobby's car and to this rest stop or why she had found her.

Focus on the result.

Was she inside calling for help?

Were the police or the highway patrolmen about to arrive?

Would helicopters appear in the sky and come to her rescue?

Any moment would she hear sirens and the amplified voices of authorities telling the Monster that it was all over?

They would say that he should put down the gun and step out of the vehicle.

Is that what would happen next?

* * *

Destiny was crunched low, with her butt right on her heels.

She could see the door open on the driver's side and then, seconds later, the door on the passenger's side angled wide. But she was at the wrong angle to follow what was happening.

She edged higher up and caught sight of Emily Bell being led behind the silver car, where they both disappeared from view.

44

Sam now drove. Bobby Ellis spoke to the OnBoard technician.

Sam kept his eyes on the highway, but he saw Bobby's chin move up and down. He was listening and seemingly agreeing with someone.

And then Bobby said: "Thank you. I appreciate it. You've got my number. You can call back if there are any changes."

Bobby pressed a button on his cell phone and ended the call. "The car hasn't moved in five minutes. It looks like it's in a rest stop."

Sam took his eyes off the road to look at Bobby. "Call the police."

"We don't need to do that."

Sam's voice got louder. "Yes, we do. Call them."

Bobby shook his head. "We'll be there in less than thirty minutes."

Sam was yelling now. "Just call! Do it! *Call the police!*"

"It's not the police. We're not in a city anymore. The jurisdiction would be state troopers."

Sam reached for his cell phone. "So we call state troopers!"

But before he could do that, his own phone rang. Sam looked down at the digital display.

He knew that number. It was the Bell house.

He felt his heart inside his chest fold inward with relief.

This was it.

It was Emily calling from home. Right here would be the explanation. And this nightmare would all be over.

Sam pressed the button and heard Riddle's voice. It was tight. Low. Barely audible. "I think Dad got out of jail. I think he's trying to get us."

* * *

They stood at the back of the silver car with the trunk now popped open, and Emily was struck by the sound that the wind makes when it blows pine trees.

She'd heard it her whole life. A gentle swooshing.

The needles rub up against one another and create a rustling noise that a person never forgets.

Would she remember this day with the sound of the pine needles?

Would she live to have that experience?

Focus.

On.

Details.

If she could see every single thing around her, every small detail, that meant that she was, in fact, alive.

He had one hand on her upper arm. He gripped it. Very hard.

She knew that there would be bruises in two places: where his thumb dug into the inner portion of her arm, and on the outside, where his other fingers took hold.

He had one hand on her. And one hand on the gun. The heat coming from inside the trunk could be felt several feet away.

She glanced down and saw camping stuff.

A tent. A sleeping bag. A tarp. It was all neatly packed. She also saw a tennis racket.

She couldn't picture the Monster playing tennis. Underneath the racket was a pair of white tennis shoes. But they were small. With hot pink fabric lining the inside. They were women's shoes.

They must belong to the person who owned the car. The stolen car. She hoped the owner was still alive. And searching for her Honda.

But Robb Ellis's SUV was parked in this lot, and Destiny was somewhere in the cinder-block building, and that had to mean people were coming to help her.

Then the Monster holding the gun said, "Get in."

She couldn't stand to see his eyes. She saw Sam in those eyes. So she stared at the ground as she asked: "You want me to get into the trunk?"

His voice was hard. "Right now."

She still had her purse over her shoulder. He suddenly released his grip on her arm and ripped the purse off her body. And for a brief moment, that felt like a violent assault worse than being forced into a trunk.

261

That was her purse. It had her things. Her useless cell phone and her wallet with her ID. Without her identification, how would anyone ever know who she was?

He flung the purse into the bushes and grabbed her arm so hard, it felt as if he were going to break it. The purse no longer mattered.

Gone.

She smelled alcohol on his sour breath as she heard: "Get in the trunk right now."

She lifted her right leg into the back and then lowered her body, which felt like someone else's, as she climbed into the dark space.

In order to be able to fit, she had to bring her legs up to her chest and, for a moment, she thought he was going to slam the lid of the trunk straight down on her head.

She wasn't yet crunched up enough to fit into the space. She cringed, but he didn't hit her.

It was just a threat.

She pulled herself together and then put her head down on a hot nylon bag, which held the tent. She felt a metal pole against her ear.

And then the Monster banged the lid shut, which plunged her into darkness.

* * *

She heard the electronic chirp and the click of the car locks sucking into place.

She had her legs folded up so close to her body that her chin rested on her sweating knees. It was the crunch of a fetal position.

She was going back to being unborn.

Was the first step in dying returning to darkness and the crammed place where someone else did the breathing?

Her chest had difficulty rising and falling, expanding and contracting.

It wasn't just how hot the air was. Or how compressed her body felt in the metal container that was the trunk of a new-model Honda sedan.

It was more than that.

She suddenly felt certain that this was her coffin.

She decided that this was what it must feel like to be conscious when they put you in the final resting place.

Her lips moved to form a single word.

Destiny.

* * *

She couldn't see Emily.

But the tall man with the coppery hair had shut the trunk. She could see again. He was now walking away from the car. And he had something in his hand as it slid into his pocket.

Was it the gun?

He moved toward the bathroom, which meant he was coming toward her. He had a limp. She understood from his twisted face that something was causing him pain.

Destiny remained frozen at the back corner of the building.

As the man came closer, something about him looked familiar.

He had strange-colored hair and a choppy haircut, and his jaw was set at an angle that showed tension, even from a distance.

Destiny took a deep breath.

Well, he didn't scare her.

She exhaled.

Okay.

He did scare her.

He totally scared her.

But she hadn't struck out on her own as a kid by being scared.

Or maybe she had.

So maybe she had used fear to her advantage. That was another way to see it.

She could feel her heart pounding, and her sweat made her dress stick to her now as if spray-on adhesive had been applied to her body.

* * *

He entered the cinder-block crapper, and it was quiet.

Maybe the girl had flushed herself down the toilet.

He had to use the facilities, and suddenly she was nothing to him. Just another person who didn't believe a sign that said *Closed* meant anything.

Or maybe she was some kind of junkie, and she'd shot up and was now slumped over in a stupor in a dirty stall.

He hoped that she had overdosed.

Clarence went around the privacy wall that led to the men's area and was greeted by the institutional toilets that were exactly like those in prison.

He was surprised that just the sight of the stainless steel brought up a wave of hate that crashed over him hard.

That pain felt like electricity running down an exposed wire touched by his open hand.

He felt dizzy.

His ache was so deep.

He would share the feeling with the world.

*　*　*

Destiny looked across the hot blacktop of the parking lot, and heat was making wavy lines that were shaking everything.

It wasn't now or never.

It was maybe now. Maybe never.

What was she even doing here?

A voice inside screamed that she was there for a reason. She had to do something. She was the kid who jumped into the cold pool. She never stuck her toe in first.

And then a switch was flipped, and she took off at a run. It was as if she were on fire.

The big rig. That was the answer. That was where she would find help.

When she reached the truck, she grabbed the chrome handle next to the driver's-side door and hoisted herself up.

But the door was locked.

Destiny's fist pounded the hot glass.

It was silent inside.

Not a sound.

And no one in sight.

Destiny's head whipped back to the cinder-block bathroom.

He hadn't come out.

She then jumped down from the step below the driver's door. Hitting the pavement hard, she took off again in a sprint.

This time she ran for the silver car.

The distance seemed great because she felt so exposed. When she reached the Honda, she was out of breath. She could see that no one was inside, but her hand still went for the door handle on the passenger's side.

Locked.

Nothing. Nothing. Nothing.

So where was Emily?

In frustration she made a fist and hit the trunk.

And then from inside something hit back.

* * *

It was dark and roasting hot.

And it smelled like dirt.

The tent wrapped up in the nylon sack had been in the

campsite for three days, and the outdoors was now a part of the baking upholstery. The tennis racket and the tennis balls, pushed over next to the spare tire, also had a distinctive odor.

She hadn't been inside for long, and she already felt as if she were suffocating.

And then suddenly, in this tomb, there was a sound.

A thud. Just above her head.

But it didn't seem like the thud that the Monster would make. It was a pop. A small hand?

Should she scream at the top of her lungs for the world to hear?

Instead she made a fist with her right hand, and she had only a few inches of available motion, but she hit back. Not a thud but a bump.

And then she heard a muffled voice: "OhmyGod! Emily?"

It was Destiny.

Emily opened her mouth to answer, and she tried, but her voice was closed down, and the tightness in her throat released only the smallest of sounds. Only a murmur:

"Help me...."

* * *

The trunk of the silver car was locked.

Destiny looked up at the cinder-block bathroom.

He was coming.

She couldn't see him. But she knew.

He was coming. He had to be.

Destiny grabbed each of the doors' handles and tried again, even though it was obvious to her this was a waste of time.

But if she could get a door open, she would find the release to the trunk. Inside would be a lever.

And then she saw the stack of cinder blocks on the other side of the parking lot. They were next to the piles of sand and gravel.

Destiny took off across the blacktop, running to the cinder-block stack.

Her legs felt like rubber. They didn't belong to her. She was someone else now.

Destiny picked up a cinder block. It was much heavier than she'd thought. The cement edge tore at her hand when she grabbed it. She barely felt her skin rip.

She tried to run back to the car, but she was small and the cinder block was heavy. She gripped it with both hands, trying to hold it in front of her legs.

All the while was the knowledge that he was coming.

The cinder block hit her thighs and slammed into her knees. She was bleeding from her hand and from her right leg as she approached the silver car.

Then, using all the strength in her upper body, she threw the cinder block at the window on the passenger's side.

It hit with a violent crash, and the glass fell like a sheet. It looked like broken diamonds glistening on the seats.

The car alarm was blaring now. And it seemed like the whole world could hear.

45

He'd done his business.

He winced as he turned to go, because his missing foot hurt. It was because it was so hot outside. The heat irritated his skin, and his artificial leg made him sweat even more than normal.

He needed to cool down the stump.

The sinks were too high, and there was no way to get his body up to the right angle. But once he had a thought, he became obsessed. Now the thought was cold water on the scarred nub.

The girl was locked in the trunk. He'd taken care of that. Time was on his side.

There were metal toilets, just like in his cell. They looked okay. If he dropped in paper towels and then flushed multiple times, the bowl would fill up with cold water.

So why not? He'd done it before.

The place looked sanitary enough because it was closed

and maybe they'd cleaned it. It wasn't spotless, but he wasn't going to really look. He was thinking fuzzy now. The alcohol and the pills and the drive were numbing.

Some other man's piss could wash over his stump, if that's what it took to make his hacked-away foot stop screaming for attention.

And so he dropped a handful of brown paper towels into the stainless-steel toilet bowl, and then he shifted his weight onto his good foot and flushed three times in a row, sending jets of cool water into the basin.

Leaning against the metal divider of the cubicle, he bent over. He was a below-the-knee amputee. If the government weren't in charge, he could have gotten a foot that had toes. Or that had skin color that matched. He could have had it shaped and customized.

But that stuff cost money, and he wasn't getting state-of-the-art rich-man care.

His stump was covered with a silicone liner. Every morning, when he put on the leg, he rolled the liner over the stump, making sure he didn't tear the oozy rubber. It had to fit just right or he couldn't lock in the socket.

Over the liner he had a rubbery sock that had a steel rod. He had to position it just right or it wouldn't click into the dummy. The dummy was the leg-and-foot part.

The dummy was so dumb, he often thought, that it couldn't tell the missing foot to shut up and stop screaming.

Getting it off was easier than putting it on. But he had it down now. What once was a difficult process was now just a series of motions.

Clarence released the pin, rolled down the sock, pulled it loose, and then removed the liner.

One. Two. Three. Four.

He then dropped the stump into the toilet bowl, and the cool water touching the rash of red skin sent tingles up his leg and into his spine.

And a split second later, he heard the sound of breaking glass and the car alarm.

Clarence grabbed his artificial leg and began furiously trying to put the pin back into the socket of the prosthesis.

He struggled in what was now a crazy man's rage.

*　*　*

K.B. Walton's eyes opened, and his first thought was that someone was going after his rig.

He had a full load: auto parts to be moved across the country for a brake recall. It wasn't like transporting a truck weighed down with flat-screen televisions, but those brakes were worth real money. And thieves didn't necessarily know what they'd get when they went after someone's haul. They made mistakes just like everyone else.

Trucking pirates were the reason that Walton kept a gun right behind the front seat. It wasn't legal in every state, but being a trucker, what worked in one place was off-limits somewhere else.

So you had to turn a blind eye.

Now, as he pulled himself up off the cot, his body half

numb and tingling, he expected to see his windshield or one of his windows busted up.

But they weren't.

K.B. moved stiff and jerky like a robot with low batteries as he made his way to his feet. How long had he been asleep?

From the heat inside the truck cabin, a long time. It was stuffy, and the fan had gone off. He suddenly felt like he was baking alive.

It had been dark when he'd pulled over. And now the sun was high in the sky. What was up with that?

K.B.'s neuropathy was messing with him now. Half of his body wasn't cooperating.

He reached down to the toolbox where he kept the gun, and he couldn't get it open. His hand felt like a crab claw trying to pick up a single strand of silk thread. He was thrashing to get his fingers to even bend.

And then, at long last, the toolbox popped open.

His three fingers found the gun, but his upper arm felt numb, and he couldn't raise his hand more than a foot. So the gun hung at his side, a weapon that would be useful if he were shooting at the dirt.

He considered the sound again.

Maybe what he'd heard was a trash can with bottles that had tumbled over.

A bear? A coyote? The wind? All kinds of stuff happened.

It didn't have to be something wicked in the parking lot.

But K.B. forced himself forward, gun dangling limp from his deadweight arm.

* * *

Destiny reached her hand through the open cavity and grabbed the door lock, pulling up. She then flung the door wide, her eyes searching all the while.

And then she saw it.

The latch to open the trunk.

It was on the floor. Destiny put a knee on the seat, a knee that crushed right into the glistening, corn-kernel-size chunks of the safety glass.

They looked like ice on the black upholstery. She didn't feel a thing as the shards stuck like gravel into the pink skin of her bony kneecap.

Pop.

It was open. Destiny ran to the back, screaming now:

"Emily!"

But Emily was already climbing out, her hands clawing at the trunk lid like something wild released from a cage. She was panting, rapid puffs as if she'd been running, when instead she'd been curled up in a ball in the hot dark.

And then Destiny saw him.

Emily looked over at the same instant.

The Monster was out of the cinder-block building.

* * *

K.B. Walton opened the back door of his big rig cab.

The air outside was warm and heavy, but it was still a welcome relief from the stuffy interior of his truck.

If only he could get some circulation back into his arms and legs.

He was able to find the handrail that he'd attached to the back panel three years before, when things first started to go tingly in his world. Now he was grateful as he lowered himself down the two metal steps.

K.B. touched the blacktop just in time to see a man step out of the cinder-block structure across the parking lot. He looked like he had a gun in his hand.

What's going on?

K.B. could see two things right away: the man walked with a limp and with a sense of purpose. His face looked enraged.

As a trucker, K.B. Walton had seen all kinds of trouble. And what he'd learned was to stay away from another man's problems. He had enough of his own.

K.B. swung back around, with the intent of returning to the cab of his big rig, and then he heard female voices.

One of them was shouting.

That was when K.B. saw the silver car. And the two girls. They looked terrified.

He couldn't hear clearly what the girls were saying, but the cries were for help. That much he could figure.

Walton turned back to the man.

There was a black SUV parked just outside the cinder-block building, and the orange-haired man now pointed his gun at the front left tire of the car and fired.

The shot sounded like the bang of an exhaust pipe.

A loud boom followed by a muffled *pfffttt* as the bullet pierced the rubber.

Walton watched as the man calmly took aim a second time at the SUV's right front tire and pulled the trigger again. A second bang pierced the silence, causing that tire to lose its form.

The trucker stood frozen on the blacktop.

Now, that just isn't right.

Who does that fella think he is?

It didn't matter what someone had done to you; you don't go shooting out a person's tires.

And then the orange-haired man turned his head and saw him.

His gaze went from the girls, who were crouched nearby, behind the silver car, to the big rig.

And that was when the man started across the asphalt, straight toward the trucker.

* * *

Emily and Destiny held on to each other, their hearts racing and their adrenaline surging, both filled with the kind of terror that removes all rationality.

There was no time for logic.

Emily had no idea how or why Destiny was there, but the sight of the girl allowed air to return to her lungs.

Now there were two of them against him.

And then suddenly there were three.

A man—older, big, and stiff-looking—emerged from the cab of the eighteen-wheeled truck. He had on a short-sleeved shirt and fuzzy gray sweatpants that looked like pajamas.

They were far away, but Destiny opened her mouth and screamed:

"Help! *Help us!!! He's trying to kill us!*"

Most of the sound of her screaming voice disappeared into the rustling pine needles and the distant growl of the unseen highway. But bits and pieces of high-pitched distress filtered across the parking lot.

They could see now that the large man—the stiff-moving trucker—was trying to raise his right arm.

In his hand was a gun.

* * *

The Monster moved away from the black SUV and toward the big rig.

The older man struggled to take aim.

The girls watched.

But something was wrong. His arm wasn't working.

Because the Monster was able to level his gun and fire first.

* * *

This was all wrong.

Some guy just comes out of the bathroom and starts shooting at a parked car, and there are two girls who look in trouble, so this guy is some kind of lunatic.

And one of the girls, the short one who might even be a child, shouts for help.

Well, he could get help.

Or at least he would if he could move. But he could only make things go slowly now. Even with a surge of adrenaline, his limbs were weak and seemed to belong to someone else.

They failed him.

Epic fail, as his grandson would say.

His arm only raised up half the distance that he needed it to go.

And then the guy pointed his gun.

Is he aiming at the big rig?

No.

He's aiming at me.

No.

Yes.

No.

YES. Oh. Yes.

There was an explosion.

But then it was over.

A switch. Like the ignition. On and then off.

K.B. Walton had reached the end of the line.

He had a final thought as he sank to the ground.

There is a reason not to go into a rest stop when the sign says it's closed. He wished he could write a song with that title.

46

The man who came out of the truck to rescue them had been shot.

He was on the ground, and his pale blue short-sleeved shirt was turning red.

The Monster had killed a man.

Right in front of them. In broad daylight.

And now that was what he would do to the two of them.

Emily had kept it together for the entire time they'd been in the car driving. She had found a way to focus. She hadn't cried, and she'd barely moved a muscle. She had hardly made a sound.

But now she shattered into as many pieces of glass as the window of the silver car.

Emily started to shake as badly as when she had been locked in the restaurant freezer right before she was discovered. She couldn't control her own body.

Destiny grabbed hold of Emily's arm. But Emily couldn't feel her touch.

Destiny said: "We're going to run. He can't run like we can. He limps. He's got a messed-up leg."

Emily didn't think that she could even walk. Much less run.

She'd had dreams where bad people were chasing her and her legs turned to heavy, immovable parts that would not cooperate with her body.

It terrified her in her sleep, and now it was happening to her in real life.

Emily's teeth were chattering when she said, "I can't run."

Destiny watched as the evil man started toward them.

Not fast. Not slow.

Just deliberate.

Destiny sized up the parking lot.

It was too far to the unseen highway, and there was a wire fence that ran between the planted grassy area and the trees.

Maybe they could go over the fence and then cut through the trees. But the fence was too high. The fence was to keep deer from running across Route 97.

And now they were the deer.

Destiny tightened her grip on Emily. "We can't stay here."

Her eyes were on the big rig. She shouted at Emily: "We're going to the truck."

Emily shook her head but babbled, "We can't go there. That man's dead. We—"

But Destiny was in charge. "We've got to run fast. We've got to go *now*."

Emily looked at her. What was she saying? She couldn't

279

run. She couldn't even walk. She was shaking. She couldn't move.

And then Destiny's sharp little fingernails, painted bright orange and looking like bits of candy, dug into her arm, and Destiny pulled hard on Emily.

"We're not running together. It makes it easier for him to aim when it's one large thing. Just follow me. But not right behind. Not in a straight line. Go, Emily! *Go now!* Don't think, just *go*! *We're going!*"

* * *

Who was that girl?

How did she go from the crapper out to the parking lot? And why?

Why?

Why?

Why?

Why?

She broke the window and got into his car. And she had freed his girl.

She'd pay for what she'd done.

The old man in the truck had paid. Couldn't they see that?

Well, now it was their turn.

It would be a doubles game. Shoot them both. And then run over their bodies with his car.

He heard a voice inside asking: *Why do that?*

He answered out loud: "Because I can."

It would take the police longer to figure out what had happened. A truck. Three dead bodies. An SUV with flat tires.

And then the girls both took off.

They ran across the parking lot, away from the silver car to the big rig.

He didn't expect that. He expected them to cower.

To cry.

To beg.

His anger, which had already rolled itself into a compost pile of rot, now ignited into a blaze of fire.

He lifted his gun.

Bang.

    Bang.

        Bang.

You're dead.

*   *   *

The sound of the bullets echoed in the parking lot.

One.

    Two.

        Three.

But they were moving.

Emily's legs were not pillars of stone. Her legs were strong.

And they were totally in charge.

They propelled her suddenly right past Destiny, and while bullets whizzed by, she moved across the wide, open space until she was safely behind the big rig.

And that was when Destiny, several paces back, went down.

One of her little slippery silk shoes from Thailand, which were meant for a traditional ceremony in a teahouse, got stuck in a rut in the alligator-back asphalt that made up the west section of the parking lot.

Emily looked over her shoulder to see her fall. She didn't even consider the options.

Bang.

   Bang.

      Bang.

She ran back out into the open and grabbed Destiny's arm, pulling her up off the ground as the shots continued to ring out.

   Bang.

  Bang.

Bang.

Destiny's knee was a bloody mess, but not from gunfire. She'd fallen, but she hadn't been shot. She was already up on her feet.

With her first step forward, her left orange slipper flew right off her heel.

But she kept running.

*　*　*

He fired the gun, but the bullets missed the targets. His closest shot had been the first one discharged. After that, he was dealing with the recoil from the gun.

He couldn't steady himself. It was the missing leg's fault. He had trouble with his balance.

When the smaller girl went down, he thought that he had her.

But with the sun in his eyes, and his stability compromised, their movement was too much for him to be accurate.

He watched bitterly as his girl helped the small one to her feet. And then the two of them disappeared behind the truck.

Why were they doing this to him?

Why were they making it all so difficult?

*   *   *

Once behind the big rig, Emily and Destiny pressed up against one of the wheels.

Destiny's little chest was heaving like a bird's as they both struggled to catch their breath.

By looking under the truck, they could see the almost-dead man on the ground on the other side. Fluid was seeping from the back of his head. And blood soaked his short-sleeved shirt.

His eyes were open, and he was staring up at the sky, unblinking. It looked like he was resting. He might have been in a trance, gazing straight at the hot sun.

He was preparing.

Emily was transfixed as his chest suddenly deflated with a muscle spasm. It was a cough that had a gurgle mixed in, and then his body changed and was perfectly still.

And she saw the transition from life to death.

The vanishing.

She felt it inside. His body was still there, but his soul was now gone.

Right there, behind the big rig, lay a man who only minutes before had never seen her or the Monster. Now his life was over, because he'd parked his truck in the wrong place that day.

47

Destiny struggled to catch her breath. Maybe she would never again have lungs that worked right. Was that possible? Hadn't she almost just died out there?

How had Emily, the girl who lived in that perfect house with the perfect yard and the perfect driveway made of bricks set at perfect angles, gotten into this mess?

Dark-haired Emily, who had that most perfect boyfriend, now had the worst luck in the world.

Because this was just *all messed up.*

What would have happened if Emily hadn't gone back and pulled her off the ground?

Destiny might be lying out there like the dead guy on the other side of the tires.

They hadn't been hit by a bullet running from the silver car to their hiding place behind the truck, but the maniac was still out there.

Destiny tried to focus.

She did know her way around a big rig. The guy she had married, Wynn, was a driver. And she'd been one, too. She never got licensed, but she'd driven Wynn's eighteen-wheeler enough miles to feel confident behind the wheel. Hadn't Wynn said all the time that she was a natural?

She guessed that the trucker lying on the ground on the other side of the axle hadn't thought to take his keys. Destiny looked at Emily, who was still staring at him, and said, "I'm sure he left the keys inside."

Destiny moved like an acrobat. She hoisted herself up the side of the cab to the door, and it opened.

* * *

It was hot inside the truck. And it smelled like banana peels. But it also felt a whole lot more protected.

Once Emily was in, Destiny locked the door behind her. She then checked the ignition, and sure enough, that was where she found the keys.

They were looking down on their tormentor now. The view out the front windshield gave the two girls an angle on him.

Destiny's voice was high-pitched and shaky. "Who is that guy?"

Emily was going to answer "Sam's father," but the need to protect him, always, was so great that what came out was: "Satan."

Destiny was tossing things now, looking through the

mess of crap in the center console. She pushed aside coffee cups and medicine bottles.

"The trucker had to have had a cell phone—right?"

There was a GPS system. A thermos. A stack of inventory sheets. She didn't see a cell phone.

She frantically shouted at Emily, who had never taken her eyes off Clarence. "Don't you have a cell phone?"

"It's dead. No battery. I didn't charge it last night. And besides, it's in my purse, which is gone."

Destiny was shrieking now. "Help me look!"

Emily shouted back, "He's coming to get us!"

Destiny opened her mouth to say something and then *bam*.

The right panel of the windshield suddenly exploded.

The bullet pierced the glass and lodged in the metal wall behind the driver's seat.

It took only a microsecond for the whole sheet of glass to crack into a spiderweb of small chunks and then fall apart.

Both girls dropped.

Emily hid behind the front seat, and Destiny crouched in the space between the front seat and the passenger's seat, next to the gearshift.

Destiny slid over on the floor mat, which was now covered in glass. She put her bare left foot on the brake. She then reached up and grabbed the key in the ignition and turned.

"We gotta get out of here!"

*   *   *

Clarence had put the dummy on wrong.

That was the problem. He was struggling to move now, because the metal pin wasn't in right.

But he was almost there. It was going to take real effort to pull himself up into the cab of the truck, but he could do it.

And then a loud rumble echoed across the parking lot.

A cloud of black smoke belched from the tall chrome exhaust pipe running up the side of the cab as the entire truck shook to life.

Was there someone else inside the big rig besides the two girls?

He couldn't see anyone.

Half the windshield was gone, and the other side was still intact, but no one appeared to be there.

And then the truck's transmission whined as the eighteen-wheeler lurched forward.

* * *

There were ten gears, and it required a driver to double-clutch.

She'd done that before.

But there was a problem.

When she was married to Wynn, he had built her a special seat, like a kid would use in a family-style restaurant.

It pushed her forward and raised her up, on an angle, so that she could see over the steering wheel but could also reach the pedals.

288

Now she had no booster seat, and she couldn't risk half standing and being so visible. So Destiny crunched up on the floor mat, her knees against her chest, as she worked the pedals.

Once the truck made its first heave forward, Emily inched her way through the glass. "What should I do?"

Destiny pumped the clutch like an expert. "You can steer."

Emily grabbed the bottom of the steering wheel. "But I can't see!"

Destiny had all her concentration on the gas pedal. "Just turn. Maybe we'll hit him."

*　　*　　*

The truck was driving itself.

That wasn't possible, of course, but from his vantage point, that's what he saw.

He'd never even taken that second handful of pain pills, so it couldn't be some kind of hallucination.

Somehow the truck had started, and it was moving.

Now it needed to be stopped.

Clarence fired at the front tire.

Bang.

The bullet pierced the enormous rubber tire, but it didn't appear to accomplish anything, because there were two tires, side by side, and behind them, two more.

And these things didn't blow out.

They shredded and they fell apart, but they didn't explode and they didn't disable.

What the hell was that about?

The truck was turning now. It was, he realized, suddenly heading right at him.

Clarence moved to the right. But the truck continued in an arc in the same direction, and it was picking up speed.

And so he changed course and hobbled, as quickly as he could, backward.

Once Clarence had dodged out of the way, he watched as the big rig lurched into a higher gear.

It swung in a wide curve across the blacktop and then, as if aiming for a target, the huge truck slammed right into the black SUV parked in front of the cinder-block bathrooms.

* * *

Just the forward motion made them feel as if they were free.

Destiny's feet worked the clutch and the gas; she shifted by pulling low on the gear stick.

The truck was designed to go from second to third to fourth gear while not even topping twenty miles an hour. And Destiny was making that happen.

Emily pulled on the steering wheel with one arm.

They could tell that they were turning, but they had no idea of much else.

And then they hit Robb Ellis's SUV.

The sound was worse than the jolt of impact.

There was the low-pitched snarl of metal on metal mixed with shattering glass as the big rig, still going forward, pushed the crumpling SUV like a tin toy.

Emily and Destiny popped up from the floor to see.

And for a split second, they both forgot about their tormentor and their predicament.

Destiny's mouth dropped open. "OhmyGod...Robb's car."

The SUV was destroyed.

But the truck was still moving. Destiny kept her foot on the gas and turned the wheel hard.

The SUV, now a hunk of twisted metal, spun off to the side, set free.

And that was when they saw Clarence on the blacktop, with his gun aimed right up at them.

48

Both of the cats were in Riddle's lap.

Jared was next to him on the couch. Close. Beto had stayed at home.

Debbie Bell was on the phone across the room. Her husband was talking on a phone outside.

Riddle shut his eyes and tried to breathe. He took a black pen, and for the first time he didn't draw. He wrote words in his sketchbook.

We brot the bad in to this howz.

We shud be punisht.

Not Emily.

Not her.

Not now.

Not evur.

We will not sirfive with awht Emily.

She is what holds us all to this growd.

Riddle then shut the book and leaned against Jared. And in silence they were for the first time really brothers.

*   *   *

After Sam hung up with Riddle, he got Tim Bell on the phone. Emily's father called the police department.

And it took only minutes to confirm that Clarence Border was out of prison.

The dominoes were falling.

So Sam *had* seen him on the neighbors' porch at night. He had been there.

Riddle was right. There had been a man in that house next door.

Their father.

Sam had not seen or heard from Emily since the night before.

Only Nora, reached by Debbie Bell, had something to add. On her break from lifeguard duty, she had received texts.

But they made no sense. They were just jumbles of letters. That was anything but reassuring.

So the wheels of the system were now turning.

But Sam could hear a voice. It said only one thing.

Too late.

Too late.

The idea of his father with Emily was beyond comprehension. Nothing, nothing, nothing could be worse.

He pressed down on the gas as the world outside blurred.

This was what he had done. This was what Sam had brought to her world. Hadn't he known all along that if he looked over his shoulder, his father would be there?

* * *

Clarence felt like grinding his teeth until they turned to salt.

People *always* let him down.

He couldn't even count on the two girls to act like girls.

Because there was something seriously wrong with both of them.

The big rig had broken free of the SUV, but the collision didn't stop the madness because the truck was still moving.

And he could now see them behind the wheel.

The eighteen-wheeler was turning in a big loop and heading around the parking lot toward his silver Honda.

They were closing his options.

Clarence reached the car, and the passenger-side door and the trunk were still open. He pounded his fist onto the lid, and it shut.

He then climbed inside, sitting in the pile of broken glass as he fished out the keys from his pocket. In seconds the ignition turned over.

He put his foot on the gas and the car bucked forward, just as the big rig barreled straight for him.

* * *

They were screaming. Loud. Ear-splitting cries that were involuntary.

No longer crouched on the black plastic floor mats, they were both up. Destiny was on the edge of the seat, fully in control of the eighteen-wheeler.

She kept her foot depressed on the gas. "He's not getting away!"

This didn't make any sense to Emily. "But we want him to get away! We want him as far away as he can get!"

Destiny's eyes narrowed in fury. "We want him to pay for what he's done!"

With that, the big rig truck hit the back of the silver car just as it began to move.

If it had been a second earlier, she'd have slammed into him full force. But the Honda's acceleration meant that the impact was like a hungry shark preying on a smaller fish. The truck got only a taste of the tail.

The silver car spun hard, doing a full 360-degree turn as the bumper ripped right off like a torn fingernail.

Inside, Clarence gripped the wheel and spit into the dashboard as he stepped on the accelerator.

The Honda wobbled, then corrected, gathering speed as it moved across the parking lot toward the exit.

* * *

Destiny didn't think of herself as a gamer, but she'd hung out with guys who were.

And so she'd taken her turn in 3-D digital situations where she was chasing bad guys, going up and over obstacles, in pursuit of justice. Or points in the game.

Now that she and Emily were free of him, she disconnected from reality.

Fired up by a flood of adrenaline and a lifetime of disappointment and frustration, Destiny Verbeck felt the tables turn.

She could be the tormentor now.

And Emily, shouting at her side, couldn't have stopped her if she'd wanted to.

* * *

The ramp from the rest stop back to the highway was a long road lined with tall trees. A series of traffic cones marked off work being done.

Clarence hit two of the temporary barriers and sent them flying as he accelerated. He had a lightweight sedan.

The maniac girls behind him had eighteen wheels of cargo.

He was certain that he'd be out of sight before they could even maneuver the big rig onto the highway.

Now, as he merged onto Route 97, he was going above

the speed limit, which was something he loathed doing. Only amateurs got pulled over by the cops for driving too fast.

But speeding was a necessary evil.

For a second he lost his focus. In this world, he wondered, what evil wasn't necessary?

Then Clarence looked into his rearview mirror, and suddenly the unimaginable appeared.

The truck was there.

He tried to make sense of the situation. What exactly did the girls think they were doing?

And then it became clear.

While the truck was slow to gain momentum, it was a beast on the road. And right now it was hauling down the highway. The air horn was blaring, and it was gaining on him.

There was no mistaking what was happening.

The big rig was coming after him.

*　　*　　*

They were giddy.

They had survived, and in their shocked state they were no longer rational in any sense of the word. The fear that had pulsed through their veins now seemed to fuel a kind of crazed hysteria.

And they were both infected. Destiny wasn't going to back down, and suddenly the illogical seemed to Emily like the only thing to do.

Destiny had shown her how to work the air horn, and

Emily now tugged on it, sending a shock of sound into the world.

They were outlaws and they were crime fighters. They were asking for attention. They were telling the world.

They were alerting the police, the authorities, and anyone and everyone to see what was happening. They were saying, *Look at the man speeding away in the silver car.*

Destiny, half standing like a kid who has stolen her parents' car, kept her little foot pressed to the floor on the gas pedal.

And even when the semitrailer began to wobble, rocking the tractor unit so that the girls felt a vibrating shimmy, the speed of the big rig kept increasing.

Over the roar of the engine, Destiny screamed as loud as she could: "Who's in charge now?"

*   *   *

He had no choice.

He was going over ninety-five miles an hour, and everything around him started to shake.

As he went over one hundred miles an hour the steering wheel began to vibrate so strongly that he was having trouble holding on.

And then the highway curved.

He tried to curve with it.

But it wasn't possible.

As he lost control the silver Honda flew out of the lane and caught the end of a guardrail.

If it had hit the structure even a foot earlier, the outcome would have been different. The metal band would have deflected the impact to the concrete posts.

But he struck the tip of the safety structure.

This section of metal bent down into the blacktop. It was the end of the line; it absorbed nothing and acted as a kind of springboard.

The Honda collided with the railing at its weakest point and was launched. Clarence and the vehicle rocketed out into the open space, traveling more than fifty yards and then slamming into the volcanic hillside.

The car then flipped and rolled down the embankment like a smashed toy.

But the journey wasn't over.

The mountainside dropped off, and the Honda fell again, only this time it disappeared entirely from view.

The tangle of twisted metal finally came to rest deep in the ravine.

*　*　*

Destiny took her foot off the gas.

She, too, had to deal with the bend in the roadway.

Experience told her that the brakes weren't going to be enough. So she applied the clutch and, double-pumping, downshifted like a pro, moving her foot on the pedals as she expertly slowed ten tons of moving metal.

And where Clarence had failed, Destiny succeeded.

She blew, too, out of her lane, but skimming along the

edge of the guardrail, sparks flying from metal on metal, she stayed in control of her vehicle.

She wasn't afraid.

She felt powerful.

All the while she could hear the voice of a video game saying, "This is the last dance for Lance Vance."

So maybe it was worth playing mindless arcade games for all those hours.

Maybe there was something to be learned from spending time in a virtual world.

49

Sam was driving faster than he'd ever traveled on a highway.

And all he wanted was for a state patrol officer to pull them over.

But no one who could help materialized.

Bobby kept his eyes on the pulsing dot of the GPS on his cell phone. "Slow down. We're almost there."

Since the revelation of Sam's father's escape, the two boys had barely spoken.

Sam put on the brakes. The two boys stared at the phone screen.

Their location and the dropped pin from the OnBoard transmitter were now the same.

But Bobby's SUV wasn't on the side of the highway. Instead, the two boys saw the sign for the rest stop. Sam put on his turn indicator. "It must be in there."

Bobby stared at the sign. "But it's closed."

Sam pulled off, following the curve of the access road.

As they entered the parking lot they were confronted with two devastating things.

They saw Bobby Ellis's destroyed SUV up on the curb by the cinder-block bathroom.

And thirty yards away, an elderly man lay on his back on the asphalt in a pool of dark liquid.

There were three oily-looking crows, several feet from the body, staring as if they were old-school crime reporters.

Bobby's hand went to his mouth. "OhmyGod!"

Sam slammed on the brakes, and the car skidded to a stop. The boys got out and started for the body, but Sam knew right away.

The guy was gone. Sam had seen a dead body before. More than once.

Bobby started to breathe in short, shallow gulps and then turned away, losing the contents of his stomach.

Sam's eyes shifted focus from the dead man to something on the ground in the middle of the parking lot. He saw an orange slipper.

Sam went for it.

He was certain it had belonged to Destiny.

* * *

Sam bellowed as if he'd lost an animal and it would appear if he called with enough urgency in his cries:

"Emily! Emily! Em-il-y!"

But the swaying pine trees swallowed up his voice, and no one responded.

Sam ran across the parking lot to the cinder-block bathrooms as he continued to shout, using all his lung power.

"Emily!"

He disappeared into the building. Three stalls. Each one with a door partially open. No one there.

He bolted to the men's side. Two stalls and a urinal. Empty. He shouted anyway.

"Emily!"

Sam emerged from the building to find Bobby sitting on the curb, crying.

The alarming sight of Bobby Ellis falling apart shook Sam into a new reality.

The air, he realized, smelled like smoke. The sky had gone from blue to milky white. Small particles of ash were falling from above.

Death was all around them now.

He had imagined multiple scenarios for what they'd see, and this was just so much worse than anything he'd come up with.

Sam pulled the cell phone from his pocket and hit three numbers. It was only a few second before he was saying:

"This is an emergency...."

50

Clarence smelled gasoline.

He opened his eyes and realized he was staring at a tree. But it was growing the wrong way. It was upside down.

He shut his eyes and tried to center himself.

Literally.

His head felt like it might explode.

Clarence worked to steady his gaze.

He was in what was left of the Honda. He was wedged in at an angle in the front seat. Upside down. Tight. Like the car had been dropped into a giant trash compactor.

As his eyes focused he could see that each piece of plastic and metal and molded-to-fit machinery was now smashed. It had all been compressed and collapsed.

Everything was destroyed.

Except him.

He was, he thought, the greatest crash dummy of all time.

Because he felt certain that he could still put two and two together and get five by taking something that wasn't his.

And then he tried to move.

His leg was trapped.

And he realized that there was a day when having lost a limb just below the knee was an advantage.

If surgeons hadn't sawed off his left leg, it would have been crushed, because his artificial limb was now garbage.

Clarence inched his fingers down to below his knee and released the metal pin. His dummy was being left behind.

He then began a process. He wiggled and squirmed, sucking his breath in and out as he shifted his position by fractions of an inch. He was a snake slithering through the smallest of openings.

He knew that staying in the car meant one thing. Smoke was rising from what was left of the engine.

He may have survived slamming into a mountain and rolling down a hillside, but he wouldn't last long in a car that went up in flames.

*   *   *

His jaw was throbbing, and he gathered the liquid in his mouth and spit. A bloody molar landed on what had been the front seat. He hoped it was the tooth that ached every morning when he woke up.

Right now everything on his body hurt, so it was impossible to tell.

Clarence felt the side of his head. His left ear was torn away from his skull and dangled as a mess of crushed flesh against his neck. He grabbed the cartilage and pulled off what remained of the flap of tissue.

That was better.

Even if it meant more bleeding.

As he gasped for air he felt certain that one of his lungs was punctured.

Covered in sticky sweat, with blood leaking from his skull, Clarence wormed his way to freedom.

He didn't have his dummy, and he wasn't sure he could stand, even if he had. But he was in one piece as he dragged himself away from the wreck. And that's all that mattered.

He was alive.

When he was only a short distance from the smoking Honda, what was left of the six-month-old sedan exploded into a fireball.

The heat burned his eyebrows and singed all the hair from his arms.

Even his eyelashes were crispy.

The coppery curls on top of his head had fused into what felt like a hairnet.

Then smoke thickened around him, changing color from black to white.

Clarence looked back to see that the brush on the uphill side of the silver car had ignited.

He stared, dry-eyed and unblinking, as the blaze later known as the Bear Paw Fire spread up the mountainside.

51

It was a windy day. And that made the difference.

The undergrowth in the forest, called "dog hair" by loggers and "fire ladder" by people who had to combat blazes, was thick in the area. It had been a mild winter and an early spring, and the vegetation had turned to the equivalent of straw.

The fire, hopscotching from the burning Honda, had an easy time unfolding in all directions. The breeze coming from the west drove it straight up the hill toward the highway.

The smoke turned the light orange.

It was as if a gauzy ginger curtain had been pulled in front of the sun.

*   *   *

Emily looked over at Destiny, who had pushed herself away from the steering wheel and was slumped deep into the driver's seat.

Moments before they had been victors.

But now they sat in silence for five minutes. They had returned to being victims.

Emily found her voice and managed to whisper, "Did we just run him off the road?"

Destiny stared through the empty windshield. "He did that to himself."

Emily took in a deep breath. She could see the column of rising smoke in the distance. "There's a fire. Down below where his car went over."

Destiny had to pull herself up to get a better look. Adrenaline still pumped through their bodies, but they were emotionally crashing. Hard.

"I guess he really messed with the wrong two girls."

Emily stared at her hand. It was shaking. She realized that her knees were hitting each other. By looking at the side mirror, she could see the back of the big rig. It took up part of the lane behind them.

"We're on a curve. We should move the truck. And we have to go back to the rest stop. We left that man there. We have to tell people."

Destiny nodded as Emily continued: "We have to report the car crash, and now the fire."

Destiny turned the key in the ignition, and the big rig fired to life. "Maybe you should make us a to-do list."

Emily took the suggestion literally. "First thing is go back to the dead man."

Destiny added, "And then we report that your kidnapper crashed his car."

"And we think that when he plunged into the gorge, it might have started a forest fire."

Destiny put the truck into gear. "Did we forget any other disasters?"

Little tears formed in the corners of Emily's eyes. "You hooked up with my boyfriend. That seemed like a catastrophe at the time."

Destiny's face fell. "Correction: I *tried* to hook up with Sam. I admit that. But I got nowhere. I climbed into his lap and couldn't make it happen. On any level."

Emily looked doubtful. "Really?"

Destiny nodded again. "After everything we've been through, you think I'd lie to you?"

Emily shrugged. "You saved my life. You're entitled to all kinds of bad behavior."

Destiny found the hazard lights on the console and flipped the switch, sending everything on the outside of the truck blinking. "Up until today, all I had was bad behavior. Maybe I just turned the corner." Then she looked down at her feet. She was wearing only one orange slipper. "I left my shoe back in the parking lot. I hope it's still there."

"I'll buy you another pair when we're back home."

Destiny's eyes suddenly glistened. "I don't have a home."

Emily's look said it all. "You do now."

Destiny grabbed the air horn as she maneuvered the big rig off the shoulder and onto the highway.

The sound blasted through the surrounding forest.

They would have to go thirty-two miles before they would reach the first place where the big rig could be turned around.

52

It was pure luck that Clarence found the train tracks.

He wasn't looking for anything other than a cave or a creek.

And then he saw the sharp metal stakes that supported the railroad ties.

The next thing he knew, he was staring at a long line of track that snaked uphill after dipping down through the ravine.

The smoke from the fire drifted against the slope, making it appear as if the whole valley was shrouded in yellow fog. That same smoke caused the freight train, part of the Burlington Northern Sante Fe line, to slow.

It had been an uneventful day for the engineer in the BNSF locomotive. At least until he reached Bear Paw Ravine.

It wasn't the first time he'd been the one to spot a forest fire.

Smoke, dense and swirling, was rising from the pit of the gorge. The tips of orange flames could be seen licking the tops of the freshly roasting pine trees.

Carefully reducing the speed of the long, heavy line of boxcars, the engineer brought the train to a complete stop.

He then dropped a GPS pin on his exact location and quickly snapped photographs. Moments later he let the world know that there was a fire in the forest.

He wasn't able to see the wreck that had started the problem.

With the temperature hot and the wind blowing from the north, the recipe for a major forest fire was in place, unless something was done.

*　*　*

Clarence Border could never have chased a moving train.

But these railcars were slowing. And then he watched as the whole line came to a stop.

Almost right in front of him.

The smoke was thickening, and at first he believed he was imagining it all.

Maybe the train was from heaven, sent to take him to the higher place?

It was so inspiring that he got to his feet. He could stand. He was dizzy but upright, now minus his dummy.

His hearing wasn't working, and his ears were ringing. But his vision didn't fail him.

He wanted to touch the metal of the powerful machine. And so he hopped forward. Moving in wobbly lurches and leaps.

Clarence reached out and grabbed the metal ladder that was positioned on the back of the closest cargo car.

It was real.

The letters BNSF were written on the side.

They were written for him.

Border Never Surrenders for ... anyone.

This train had come just to pick him up. It would carry him away. It would take him home.

Clarence summoned all the strength in his battered body and started up the ladder of the railcar, pulling himself rung by rung to the top.

The smoke was making it impossible to breathe. His stump of a leg throbbed. And blood dripped more heavily down his neck, from where he once had an ear.

But a surprise awaited him on the last rung. The railcar had a peel-back top.

Clarence unhooked a strap and pushed the tarp aside. Only a madman, he thought, would have the strength to keep going. He tumbled inside, landing in a full load of grain. It was as if he'd fallen onto a warm beach. His head settled into what felt like a giant beanbag chair.

And then the train began to move.

Someone was looking out for him.

Yes.

The blood from his many cuts and abrasions soaked the golden kernels of wheat, forming a pink outline around his body.

Clarence tilted his head to the side and realized that, if he moved his arms, he could make an angel in that grain.

Didn't he always leave his mark on the world?

His last thought as he lost consciousness was of the two girls. He hoped that they'd gone over the edge, too.

*　*　*

The dispatcher for the Oregon State Police had said to remain calm. Help was on the way.

While they waited for law enforcement to come, Sam searched every inch of the rest stop.

He ran to the trees by the highway. He moved through the tall grass near the gravel, all the while terrified that he might find something.

Another shoe.

Clothing.

Or worse.

While Sam combed the grounds, Bobby Ellis took a blue tarp that was folded up in the work area next to the cinder-block pyramids.

More crows had gathered by the dead man's body, and Bobby got the feeling that it wouldn't be long before the birds figured out a way to make a meal out of a homicide.

He lifted the plastic sheet into the air and it flapped in the dry wind. The sound caused more anxiety as he placed it over the dead man.

Moments later, Bobby found a seat on a picnic table near the cinder-block bathrooms. He tried to imagine what had happened, but it was too confusing. His wrecked car. A dead body. Destiny's orange slipper.

It took a long time for Sam to stop shouting Emily's name. He eventually quit searching in areas where he'd already looked multiple times. He finally took a seat next to Bobby Ellis.

And then he lost control.

He had never broken down like this. The world had come apart. And it was his fault.

Sam put his head between his knees and sobbed.

What had his father done?

Whatever happened next, he would need to go back and get Riddle. And then they would travel south. He could find some kind of job. Maybe he'd just play his guitar on the street for money.

But he would get Riddle into school. They would change their names. They would spend the rest of their lives righting the wrongs. They would never succeed, but they would disappear.

The only thing that he could give the Bells was the assurance that they would never have to see his face again.

*   *   *

A helicopter flew by overhead.

It was red and black and appeared to be official. They both looked up with the expectation that it might simply land at their feet.

But it kept flying.

With each passing minute, smoke from the nearby forest fire thickened. The wind was blowing harder, and before long it was impossible to see from one side of the parking lot to the other.

Sam was already having trouble breathing. The smoke made him choke on every inhale.

And then, his head downcast, he heard the noise of an approaching vehicle.

They couldn't see it, but they could hear.

Whatever was coming into the rest stop was big. The engine had a roar that broke through the eerie stillness.

Sam looked up and saw a chrome exhaust pipe belching dark smoke, which mixed with the soup of the forest-fire blaze.

An eighteen-wheeled big rig appeared as a moving mass cutting through the haze.

It looked more like a freight train than a truck.

*   *   *

Sam's eyes had to be playing tricks on him.

Through the smoke, he could make out the silhouette of two girls. The smaller of the two was driving.

And he knew.

The one in the passenger's seat had dark hair that brushed the top of her shoulders.

He couldn't see her large eyes. Or her athletic legs. Or her curling toes.

But he didn't have to.

Emily Bell, with Destiny at her side.

And they were both alive.

*   *   *

Sam wanted to tell her that he would have waited his whole life for her to come back to him.

He would have looked for her in every dawn. And in every star-filled night. He wanted to say that he was lost without her. And that his broken heart would have stayed that way forever.

The truck was still moving when he grabbed the handle of the passenger door and lifted himself up to the cab.

He had the door open, and as Destiny put on the brakes he took hold of Emily.

And all he could manage, over and over again, was to whisper through his tears.

"I'm sorry...."

*   *   *

The rest stop looked different as they rounded the curve into the parking lot.

Smoke hung in the air, and the horror of the day flooded the place so that it wasn't just a crime scene. It was the return to hell.

It had to have been someone else who had a gun shoved in her back and who had sat in that car in silence with the Monster driving.

It was another person who got locked in the trunk. Someone else had dodged a hailstorm of bullets.

And then she saw Sam. Bobby was with him. They were both running.

The next thing she knew, Sam was inside the truck.

It was only then that she returned completely.

This is me now.

Here.

With you.

This is us now.

*   *   *

None of them could remember much more about the rest of that day.

It all disappeared into a jumble of mostly questions.

Emily tried to answer, but not much came out. She held Sam's hand, and she stayed close to Destiny.

In bits, stopping and starting, they told the story.

They would do that many times. For many different people. And with each telling, the events became more distant, until the characters were not people they knew. For Emily the afternoon would begin to vanish, because she chose to let all the details disappear.

It wasn't long after the arrival of the big rig that the first highway patrol officer pulled into the rest stop.

He was followed by six other patrol cars.

And then later by Tim and Debbie Bell.

And finally a coroner's van.

* * *

The authorities were notified in California.

The prevailing theory was that Clarence Border had been hiding somewhere close to Merced, and a kind of panic had seized the community.

Now the citizens felt a deep sense of relief.

The investigation of the homicide of K.B. Walton began as soon as the truck driver's family was notified.

Emily could hear the officer breaking the news.

She shut her eyes and tried to imagine what would have happened if the man and his big rig hadn't been there at the rest stop.

She asked her mother if they could have the information to contact the trucker's family.

She wanted to make sure that his loved ones knew how grateful she was that he had come to her aid that day.

K.B. Walton had been there for two strangers. And he had paid the ultimate price.

53

A hard rain fell the day after Clarence had taken Emily.

The sudden summer cloudburst helped control the forest fire.

But the erosion from the burned hillside sent a river of mud through the crash site, and that washed away the trail Clarence had left when he'd dragged his body from the wrecked car.

It wasn't until thirty-six hours later, when the blaze had been contained, that officials were able to thoroughly investigate the area.

The fire had burned liquid-hot, and the muddy Honda was just a scorched auto skeleton.

Forensic experts were brought in, and careful sifting of the area did turn up a single human tooth. Clarence Border's DNA was positively identified from that, and the burned remains of an ear.

But the most substantial finding connecting Clarence to

the crash was the melted metal pieces from the artificial leg, buried deep in the mangled wreckage.

The rain and the mudslides were the explanation given by the investigators for the absence of other bone and body fragments. It was theorized that animals could have taken off with whatever else remained of his body.

As far as law enforcement was concerned, Clarence Border had officially died in the crash at Bear Paw Ravine.

*   *   *

Sam and Riddle sat together outside and wept at the picnic table in the Bells' backyard when they got the news.

Their tears were only of joy that their father was dead.

Riddle's voice was barely a whisper. "Sam, we won't have to go to court now—right?"

Sam nodded. "We don't have to go to court. Or talk to the police about him."

Riddle leaned into his brother. "Ever again."

Sam answered: "Emily won't have to do that either. And Destiny doesn't have to tell her part in the story."

Riddle shut his eyes as Sam continued. "We get to start over now. Really begin again."

*   *   *

Bobby wasn't sure why he'd woken up and decided he wanted to see Sam. He tried to figure out the reason as he biked over to the apartment.

They'd found the dead trucker. That was big.

And he and Sam had spent the longest day of their lives together. Or at least the longest for Bobby.

Plus, they had Emily and Destiny in common. The girls had both made it obvious that they liked Sam a lot more than him, but he was still part of the picture.

Biking across town, trying to put the pieces together, Bobby saw dozens of things he hadn't noticed before. Being on a bike, he decided, wasn't all bad. His car was gone, but it was going to be covered by insurance.

Maybe, he thought, it was time to work on a new image.

* * *

Bobby stood for several minutes by the door without knocking. He could hear guitar music. At first he thought it was a recording, but then a muffled voice that he immediately recognized started to sing, and he realized what he was listening to was live.

Bobby had always imagined himself performing onstage at a wild concert in a huge stadium. He didn't want to wear leather pants or cut his hair into a Mohawk. What he wished for was a vast audience of shrieking fans.

And later maybe a magazine cover or two.

Like a lot of his fantasies, the daydreams weren't based on any kind of reality, because Bobby didn't play a single instrument.

But he recognized someone who did. So it was with real enthusiasm that he knocked on the door. The singing and guitar stopped, and Sam appeared.

"Hey, Bobby."

"Hey, Sam."

They both weren't great at small talk. They stood in silence for a few moments, and then Sam went back inside like it was natural that Bobby Ellis would just show up to hang out without calling on a Sunday morning.

Bobby looked around the small living room. It was the opposite of his parents' house. It was simple and sparse and without decoration. He could see a hallway and two bedrooms beyond. Sunlight flooded through the back window, and both of the beds were made.

Bobby always left his room a mess. His mom or the cleaning woman, Hildy, took care of that. But here was a guy who lived by himself and didn't act like a little kid about it.

Somehow that fit.

Sam took a seat on a chair, and Bobby flopped down onto the couch. "I heard you playing. You're really good."

Sam shrugged. "I have no idea what I'm doing."

If anyone else had said that, Bobby would have been certain that they were fishing for more compliments, but in Sam's case, he knew the guy was scary honest.

Bobby continued. "I never heard that song. Who's it by?"

Sam shot him a blank look. "Me."

Bobby's eyebrows arched in disbelief. "You wrote it?"

Suddenly it was as if the ceiling had split open and hot light poured down into the room and that sunbeam landed right on Bobby. "You should play for people. Record your songs. Someone should make a video of you singing."

Sam only half smiled in his direction. Bobby continued. "Maybe I could do that."

Sam didn't answer, and Bobby took that as a good sign. "I'm interested in filmmaking. My mom's got a high-def camera at her office. I don't know anything about it, but I could learn."

Sam started to laugh, which had to mean something.

And that was enough.

*   *   *

Destiny had a new phone that had a hot-pink cover. Emily had bought it for her.

And then the Bells added her to their family plan.

But what really made Destiny feel that she belonged was when Emily took her to the library. Destiny had never been inside one before. At least not that she remembered. Seeing her name and the address of the Bells' house right there on the front of her library card made her scream. This single piece of plastic showed the world that she was for real.

It was while looking at books on careers that Destiny got the idea for what she wanted to do with her life.

She could see herself with a badge and a gun and a car with a swirling light. She wanted to chase down bad guys and put them six feet under. Or behind bars.

Especially if they had anything to do with hurting kids.

She would need to start by getting her high school equivalency. That would lead to community college and then regular college and then hopefully a police academy.

Emily made high school sound like an interesting place. Destiny had told everyone that she was twenty, but she wasn't. And she looked fifteen.

Bobby Ellis was begging her to enroll so that they'd all be seniors together.

It was now under consideration. That's what Debbie and Tim Bell had said. Maybe Destiny would actually go to Churchill High School in September.

She wasn't tricking anyone into anything with this plan. Everything was right out on the table.

* * *

Jared left the house early, because he and Beto had started a neighborhood service. They took in the mail. Fed pets. Brought in newspapers and turned lights on and off when people were vacationing.

They felt like spies because they had access to people's keys and alarm codes. And they were making money. But the best part, as far as Jared was concerned, was that he finally had Beto as a real friend.

They both had thought Riddle would want to be part of the whole thing, but he wasn't interested. He didn't want to go into the houses of strangers. He could live his whole life at the Bells' and never need to go anywhere else.

Riddle came downstairs with a book under his arm and went outside to the yard. He liked to be there in the morning. Felix and both of the cats followed him through the doorway.

He wasn't drawing as much. He was reading all the time. And he felt certain that he would do that obsessively for the rest of his life.

*   *   *

A dead man had been found in Canada. He had bled to death in a freight car filled with grain and ruined the entire shipment. There was no identification on the body, but there were several distinguishing features. There was a tattoo of a snake on a leg that had been amputated below the knee on the left side.

In the man's pocket were six prescription pain pills. And the plastic wrappers from packets of saltine crackers.

The dead body was kept in the city morgue for seventy-two hours, but then it was transferred to a county facility. Thirty days later a crematorium that had a contract with the city disposed of the remains.

Clarence Border was listed as a John Doe. No one ever came forward to claim the ashes, and the unmarked plastic bag was tossed when a cleaning crew organized a storage room. Despite legislation guaranteeing all members of society dignity in death, the cardboard box marked *John Doe* ended up in a municipal dump.

*   *   *

They were all going out for Thai food. It was Bobby's birthday, and how do you say no to someone who organizes his own party?

Emily turned on the hot water and waited the usual amount of time before stepping into the shower. But once the spray hit her legs, she knew.

Destiny.

The girl took the longest time bathing of anyone in the house. And that meant if you had to follow her, it was hopeless.

Emily decided to stay under the cold water. It was certainly a way to know she was alive. And at this point, everything that reinforced that feeling was a good thing.

There was a kind of surrender in understanding how fragile and fleeting her very existence could be.

A teenage girl who Emily barely knew had saved her life.

She now understood that the hero of her own life could at one point have been her sworn enemy. That made the whole world a more complicated place.

The day that Sam and Riddle's father had appeared was just starting to fade away. She didn't see the man behind doors or in the shadows of dark windows. But she carried a fear and apprehension she knew hadn't been there before.

She was going to overcome that. She promised herself. She just needed time. And distractions. And having Destiny Verbeck living in the room above their garage provided that. Daily.

Emily dried off with a shiver and minutes later slipped her feet into her new heels. They looked good, but Emily always found that new shoes hurt at first.

And so, she decided, did some new people. Even ones you wanted around. Even ones who had saved your life.

* * *

Sam and Bobby sat in the Bells' living room, waiting. The two girls were late. Bobby was talking about things they would do together in the future. Something about Sam playing his guitar in coffee shops.

Sam was only half listening as his mind wandered. He had let his father go. Now he could think about problems like what to get Emily for her birthday or how to sort out his class schedule in the fall. If you aren't worried about the future, he decided, maybe ideas replaced anxiety.

Sam heard the back door open and Destiny come in. She was wearing some kind of military uniform. She had on a blue jacket, blue pants, and black boots. The two boys gave each other a sideways look.

"This is the uniform of a French policewoman. What do you think?"

Bobby searched for the right words, but ended up saying, "I've seen French maid costumes. I guess those are different."

Sam jumped in. "You look nice."

Destiny didn't seem to hear either of them. "I'm not wearing it to school or anything. I'm just thinking that if I end up one day being on the police force, I should know what the outfit's like."

Bobby cleared his throat. "I think they call them uniforms. Not outfits. And are you planning on being a police officer in France?"

They all heard a voice and turned as Emily came downstairs.

327

"Happy Birthday, Bobby. Let's go get Thai food."

Destiny grabbed Bobby's arm. "Spicy? Right?"

Bobby nodded. "But not too spicy."

Sam waited till Emily got closer and then whispered to her: "She's really going to high school with you guys?"

Emily whispered back, "We'll see. My mom said it could happen."

Sam only shook his head. He reached down and scratched the dog behind the ear. He called out good-bye to Riddle and Jared, who were looking at a book on farmed fish. And then, while everyone went outside, he stuck his head in the kitchen to say good-bye to Debbie and Tim Bell.

Sam headed out the door knowing one thing for certain now. He'd spent a lot of time thinking he was cursed. But that was wrong. He'd made it through. He was the lucky one.

Sam slipped his fingers through Emily's, and they walked to where Bobby and Destiny were waiting at the end of the driveway.

The bricks on the pathway were set on an angle. They were uneven—chipped and worn from both wear and the wet Oregon weather. But as Sam went forward they were smooth under his feet.

ACKNOWLEDGMENTS

Andrea Spooner at Little, Brown was my editor, which means that this book is hers as well as mine. I thank her for being so smart, thorough, and kind. At Andrea's side is Deirdre Jones, who is going to one day (soon) be Andrea. I'm so lucky to have both of them in my life.

Amy Berkower is my agent and my friend, and if she hadn't gone into publishing, she would have been the head of the United Nations. I'm grateful she went to work at Writers House and ended up running the show with Simon Lipskar.

Ken Wright is my former agent and is now in charge of Viking Children's Books. He may think he's gotten rid of me, but he hasn't. Ever.

Tim Ellis first inspired me to write about these characters.

Alisa Allen is the woman who has my back at all times.

Lewin Wertheimer and Henry Murray led the trip that started all this.

And I want to acknowledge the following people for supporting my writing throughout the years: Geoffrey Sanford, Bob Wallerstein, Irby Smith, Dan Parada, Nadine Schiff, Joe Roth, Roger Birnbaum, John Stainton, Jan and Trish de Bont, Neal Allen, Karen Glass, Ron Burkle, Martha Luttrell, Bill Dear, Tim Goldberg, Norman Lear, Jerry Kay, Kate Juergens, Lee Smith, Darius Anderson, David Thomson, Ralf Bode, Leo Geffner, David Buelow, Matt Wallerstein, Paula Mazur, Kimberly Beck Clark, Ron Levin, Jason Clark, Rob Minkoff, David Dworski, Steve Rabineau, and Amy Holden Jones.

I write slumped with my laptop on the bed. I'm not napping, or at least not all of the time. Max, Calvin, and Gary, just call my name. I'll be there.

Everyone whose path you cross has the power to change you.

Read the beginning of Sam and Emily's story
in the following selection from

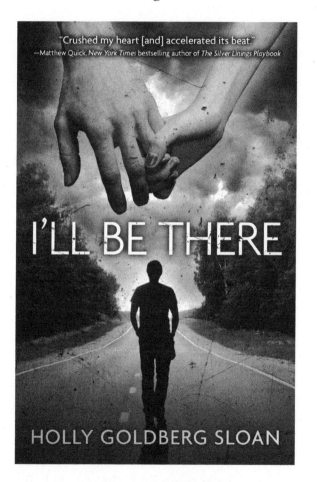

"Crushed my heart [and] accelerated its beat."
—Matthew Quick, *New York Times* bestselling author of *The Silver Linings Playbook*

I'LL BE THERE

HOLLY GOLDBERG SLOAN

Now Available

Sam's father, Clarence Border, heard voices.

But they were voices of people who were up at odd hours and who lived exclusively inside his head. They were voices of people whose jobs were primarily to warn of danger — sometimes real but mostly imagined.

When you first met Clarence Border, you understood you were talking to someone who was anxious. His thin body seemed to crackle with energy. His fingers fluttered at his sides when he spoke, moving like he was playing an invisible piano that must have been located on the tops of his bony thighs.

It wasn't that he twitched. He was more in control than that. It was that he was hardwired to run in the blink of an eye.

And to take you with him.

Clarence was a good-looking man. He had a full head of dark hair and a strong jaw. When he was dressed in his always clean black jeans, you couldn't see that on the inside of his left leg, curled around the calf, was a tattoo of a black snake. He'd given it to himself, and it looked like it.

Clarence stood over six feet tall, and you could tell in a single glance that he knew how to throw a punch — and that it wouldn't take much to get him to do it.

His voice was deep and steady, and you'd think that would be a good thing, but then his fingers would start moving and it was like he was getting a message from some far-off place, not from circuitry in his frontal lobe that just didn't seem to work right.

There are many ways Sam's father's life could have played out. He could have stayed in Alaska, living near the old cabin where he was born, hunting and fishing and on occasion taking something that wasn't his and selling it to get by. But he'd gotten caught trying to unload an outboard motor to an off-duty patrolman.

The arrest uncovered a string of other misdeeds, and Clarence found himself at the age of twenty-two in prison for three years. When he was released, he left the state, and the only thing he knew, truly deep in his heart, was that he'd never go back to living behind bars.

Which was not to say that he was going to live a life of virtue. Far from it. Clarence Border's vow wasn't one of decency. It was a vow of preservation and desperation. He'd do anything, to anyone, to keep one step ahead of the government.

For a time, life in Montana, which was where Sam was born, was without major incident. Clarence had met Shelly at the Buttrey Food & Drug store. She appeared in the aisle just as he was preparing to slip a box of cheese-flavored Goldfish crackers into the back of his bulky winter coat.

Shelly was ten years older than he was, and he could tell right away that she liked him. Since she was wearing a name tag, he just needed her phone number. She gave it to him without his even asking.

Six weeks later, Shelly was pregnant with Sam and she was living with Clarence above her parents' garage. He worked odd jobs under the watchful eye of her family, and while the whole arrangement didn't actually work, it wasn't yet a colossal failure.

Shelly's father, Donn, was an electrician. If he'd had more opportunity, he'd have been an engineer. He understood not just wiring and current and all things mechanical—he also understood operating systems.

The first time Donn met Clarence Border, he knew that his daughter had hooked up with a man who had a busted mainframe. He tried to warn her early in the game, but Shelly was pregnant before anything could be done.

Donn then took a different approach. He'd teach the shifty snake a profession. As the months wore on, a new plan took shape. If he couldn't make Clarence understand electricity, Donn could electrocute him and probably get away with it.

But the snake struck first.

The voices in his head couldn't be ignored, and the morning of the bite they told Clarence that he'd need to be righteous when someone had done him wrong.

Donn wouldn't let Clarence smoke cigarettes when they were in the truck, and when they got to the Weiss Sand and

Gravel Company, there was a No Smoking sign in the work area.

Clarence seethed as he unloaded their tools. Someone would pay for the way he was feeling.

Shelly's father was up on the roof attaching a new transformer to the pole when Clarence unhooked the ground wire. The old man was cooked in a single jolt that flung his body halfway across the roof into the company's TV dish. Smoke came off his body.

All Clarence could do was stare at the No Smoking sign and feel a sense of satisfaction.

*   *   *

After that, Shelly and Clarence moved from the garage into the main house, and Shelly's mother, consumed with grief, stopped speaking to him. He'd look back on this period as a time of focus.

When Sam was almost four and a half, Shelly got pregnant again and then, a month early, tiny Riddle was born. From the start, Riddle cried all the time. His weak sobs drove Clarence out of the house and back into the garage apartment.

The kid had colic. And some other problems. His nose ran constantly, and he squinted as if the sun were in his eyes even on rainy days. Because of his red face, Shelly named him Rudolph but he was known as Riddle from the second his father picked him up and he made his first squawk.

By the time Sam and Riddle were seven years old and

two, the house had liens and the bill collectors didn't just make calls, they paid visits.

Shelly's mom couldn't take it anymore, and even though she'd grown attached to the two little boys, she moved down to Louisiana to be with her deaf sister. She said she'd send money when she left, but no one had believed her. Clarence hadn't worked in forever, and his wife finally went back to stocking the aisles at the Buttrey.

Shelly came home after an eight-hour shift on a cold, rainy day in March and the front door was wide open. The truck wasn't in the driveway, and the garden hose by the garage was missing. Clarence had taken the two kids, some power tools, one suitcase of clothes, and her Indian Head penny collection, which had belonged to her great-uncle Jimmy.

Sam was in second grade and the star of his class, reading books for fifth graders. Ten years later, he could still picture exactly what that classroom looked like.

He'd never seen another one since.

*   *   *

Since they'd left Montana, Sam's father always told the same story. His wife had died giving birth to the young one, and then he'd lost his business. Riddle always looked like he was either just getting over a cold or just coming down with one. He'd squint out at the world, and people just naturally felt bad for the whole motherless family.

Clarence said he'd been in auto parts. Not many people

asked him about auto parts, and that was a good thing because he knew next to nothing about them.

He'd explain that he couldn't pay his employees health-care insurance premiums, but he'd chosen his workers over profit. He kept it going for as long as he could, and then finally the government came and forced him into Chapter 11.

Riddle first heard the story when he was a toddler, and back then he thought it meant that his father had been trapped inside a book. But somehow the tyrant had gotten out, and that had to be why Clarence hated teachers and any kind of learning, really.

Sam and Riddle's father believed in life experience. That's what he told the two boys. That's why he'd never let them go to school once they took to the road.

But they really didn't go to school because Clarence didn't just hate all teachers, he loathed the whole system.

*   *   *

The two boys had slept late for years. Now that they were older, their father didn't bother to even try to feed them, and they always woke up hungry.

Sam and Riddle had been taught to stay out of sight during school hours because people wanted to know why two boys were wandering around doing nothing. Plus it was better to let fast-food places open and have trash build up before they headed into the world.

They made a habit of not hitting the streets until the sun

was high in the sky and knew to say that they were home-schooled if anyone asked. But Sundays were different. Sundays, they could be seen at any time.

And Sundays there was music.

Sam pulled on his shoes and stared at his little brother, who was asleep on the stained mattress on the floor in the corner. Riddle's breathing, as always, was heavy, and his permanent congestion had the wheeze of some kind of new bronchial infection.

Sam thought about trying to prop his head up higher on the pillow because sometimes that helped, but instead he took a pen off the floor and wrote in large letters on a scrap of paper:

BE back sOON.

* * *

Sam had seen the First Unitarian Church when they originally came to town.

Was there a Second Unitarian and a Third? Was it some kind of contest?

Because now, standing in front of the brick building on Pearl Street, he could see that this house of worship was much more upscale than what he was used to. These First Unitarians were the winners. The parking lot was mostly full and the cars were new and clean, and that wasn't right for him.

This church was in the best part of town, and nothing about it looked desperate. He didn't go into places like this.

The way he saw it, the less money people had, the more instruments they played and the more food they put out. And the easier they were for him to be around.

But Sam had been all over his own neighborhood and, without Riddle at his heels, he had walked faster and somehow had ventured farther than before.

Sam had heard the pipe organ playing from down the street. It was just too intriguing. And now he could see that the First Unitarian's large wooden doors at the front were propped open.

He could get in and get out.

And maybe catch a glimpse of what was making the amazing sound.

But it wasn't that easy.

The first problem was that no sooner had Sam entered than a man appeared from nowhere and closed the oversize doors. It sounded like the closing of an entrance to a vault.

Sam slid silently into the pew in the last row. The organ stopped playing almost immediately, and a minister appeared. He wore a robe but also a tie. He leaned into a microphone and offered up some words. Sam never heard anything these people said. Instead he studied the large space.

To Sam, a room that was clean and smelled vaguely like flowers and candles was exotic. And scary. He was now giving this place his full attention.

The walls were covered in wood that looked to him like pieces of soft leather. There was a large light fixture that hung from the ceiling up front, and it had rows of tiny candles, but they weren't really candles. They would look better, he thought, if they weren't fake. But then it would be impossible to light them without a huge ladder. And also they might drip down onto people, which would be painful.

The long wooden pews were not comfortable. But they never were. If you want people to pay attention, it was important to keep them from settling in. Hadn't his father taught him that?

The man in charge finally stopped speaking, and a choir stood up from a section off to the side. The singers were all ages and shapes, wearing white robes, and they looked to Sam like birds. He didn't know the names of many types of birds, but he'd seen his share, and he felt sure that some place must have big white birds with clean feathers and hairy heads.

Then the organ again began to play, and Sam watched as a girl in the group started to weave her way through the other singers. He could see that she was his age. And he could tell, as she edged toward a microphone, that she was very nervous.

*   *   *

Emily was feeling all sweaty but sort of cold at the same time. This was just ridiculous. Her father, who was standing off to the side waving his right hand in some way that was supposed to be significant, was for sure not going to ever get any eye contact.

Once she got to the microphone, she seized on her strategy. She was going to focus on the back.

The way back.

Because that's where the people sat who checked their e-mail and monitored sports scores. The back of the church was filled with bodies that were there but not there. The nonlisteners.

Those were her people.

Or her person.

Because when she raised her eyes from the floor, she could see that today there was only one body in the last row.

Emily lifted her chin and opened her mouth and now sang directly to him:

> *"You and I must make a pact*
> *We must bring salvation back*
> *Where there is love,*
> *I'll be there"*

She could hear herself. But not hear herself. And that was the only blessing of her day. Emily knew the song. She knew the words:

> *"I'll reach out my hand to you*
> *I'll have faith in all you do*
> *Just call my name and I'll be there*
> *I'll be there to comfort you*
> *Build my world of dreams around you*
> *I'm so glad that I found you*

I'll be there with a love that's strong
I'll be your strength, I'll keep holding on
Let me fill your heart with joy and laughter
Togetherness, well that's all I'm after
Whenever you need me, I'll be there."

She was singing this all to a guy who she'd never seen before.

She could see that he was tall and thin. He had dark brown hair, which was wild and messy. Like it wasn't cut right.

The person who she was singing to was tan, like he spent a lot of time outside, even though it was still late winter.

And she realized that he looked uncomfortable. Like he didn't belong back there. Just like she didn't belong on the platform up front.

And he was intently watching her.

Pretty much everyone was watching her.

But what suddenly mattered was only that he was watching her.

Because all that had mattered to her was watching him. And now she'd made that commitment and she couldn't stop.

She was definitely giving the words of the song new meaning. Isn't that what her father had wanted? A heartfelt reinterpretation?

Was she having an out-of-body experience?

Her mouth was moving and sounds were coming out, but that didn't make sense.

What made sense was in the back row.

*   *   *

She could not really sing.

That was just a fact.

But it was also a fact that she was riveting. She was raw and exposed and not really hitting the notes right. But she was singing to him.

Why him?

He wasn't imagining it.

The girl with the long brown hair had her small hands held tight at her sides and, maybe because of how bad she was, or because she was staring right at him and seemed to be singing right to him, he couldn't look away.

She was saying she'd be there.

But no one was ever there. That's the way it was. Who was she to tell him such a thing?

It was intimate and suddenly painful.

Not just for her.

But now for him.

Very painful.

For a long time Sam was certain his mother would rescue him and Riddle.

Once she realized that they were gone, she would have called the police or the fire department (didn't they take cats out of trees?) or Mrs. Holsing, his second-grade teacher. Or even the neighbors. The ones named Natwick at the end of the street in the blue house who always waved when he walked by. People would be looking. He was sure of it.

Which of course was the case in the beginning. But his mother wasn't the kind of woman to lead an effort. She lacked not just the determination but also the organizational qualities of leadership. And it wasn't her fault.

When Shelly was a baby, her mother had placed her on the kitchen counter when she came in from the market. She'd only turned her back for a moment and the small child had wiggled free of the plastic bucket that was one of the early versions of a car seat. The straps were so complicated. Who needed them?

Shelly's head hit the floor with a thud that sounded like a bat hitting a watermelon. She was unconscious for a full five minutes, only coming around as their station wagon pulled into the emergency-room parking lot.

The doctors kept baby Shelly overnight and said everything was probably fine. The family couldn't deny that she was a loving child, calm and easy to care for. But after that day, she no longer had the potential for her father's brainpower or her mother's musical ability. If her mind was some kind of computer, that fall to the kitchen floor wiped away whole sections of her hard drive.

Once Sam's father took off with her boys, Shelly started going to My Office. The gimmick of the place was the revolving front door. There wasn't another one in town, and this piece of salvaged metal and glass, from a former savings-and-loan building in Denver, made it appear that you were really going into a place of interest.

In reality, the inside was just the corner space of the neighborhood mini-mall, and the only other attempt at an office setting was that a wall of dinged file cabinets made up the bar.

Shelly went straight there from work, which got her through the hardest time of the day. Dinner hour was when she most missed her two boys, and if she wasn't drinking, she found herself cooking for people who no longer existed.

At My Office, Shelly always sat facing the door sipping Shirley Temples because they reminded her of the kids. But her Shirley Temples had two shots of vodka dumped in with the red syrup.

Clarence had been gone for only six weeks when she got hit. She was walking home after a half dozen sweet drinks when, according to the police report, she darted out into traffic. It was impossible to know if it was suicide, an awkward street crossing, or both. She was pronounced dead on the scene. But they took her to the hospital anyway.

The nurse who admitted her body was the same nurse who had been there the day, over forty years before, when she had come in as an infant. The nurse had been young then, fresh out of school. Now she was in her sixties and had arthritis in her knees.

But she remembered.

She wrote the words *Head Injury* on the form for the death certificate and at the last minute added in parentheses *preexisting condition*. She believed in full disclosure.

Six months later, the town's local chief of police retired. The new man in charge of the department was an outsider who was all about responding to the immediate needs of the community. With no one pressing for updates on the missing boys, the case moved lower in priority.

Shelly's mother passed away from a stroke the following year and, after that, even if they had been found, there was no one to return the boys to. The missing Border children were an open file that was in reality closed.

But of course Sam didn't know that.

He imagined his mother in the old house waiting. Even in his fantasies, Shelly was never in the world looking for him. She was always sitting by the phone, staring out the window, longing for him to come through the front door and into her arms.

With time the fantasy faded, as did his image of his mother, until when he thought of her, which was rare, she was always in deep shadows, her face unseen. As the years passed, the whole house had turned dark and lost its shape.

But now, glued to the wooden pew in the back row of the First Unitarian Church, he felt an old feeling flooding over him. Sam's mother was there, somewhere, reaching out to him. She was trying to show him a way home.

Because hadn't she played this song? Hadn't she sung "I'll Be There" to him? Is that why he knew this music so well?

And with the connection, the knot, which was permanently twisted in his stomach, released.

HOLLY GOLDBERG SLOAN was born in Ann Arbor, Michigan, and spent her childhood living in California, the Netherlands, Istanbul, Washington, DC, and Oregon. She is the author of the acclaimed *I'll Be There* and *Counting by 7s* and has written and directed a number of successful family feature films, including *Angels in the Outfield*, *The Big Green*, and *Made in America*. The mother of two sons, Holly lives with her husband in Santa Monica, California.